ALSO BY
DARCY COATES

THE WHISPERING DEAD

GRAVEKEEPER #1

DARCY COATES

Poisoned Pen
PRESS

Sourcebooks, Poisoned Pen Press, and the colophon are registered trademarks of Sourcebooks.

Published by Poisoned Pen Press, an imprint of Sourcebooks
P.O. Box 4410, Naperville, Illinois 60567-4410
(630) 961-3900
sourcebooks.com

Library of Congress Cataloging-in-Publication Data

Names: Coates, Darcy, author.
Title: The whispering dead / Darcy Coates.
Description: Naperville, Illinois : Poisoned Pen Press, [2021] | Series:
   Gravekeeper ; book 1
Identifiers: LCCN 2020049756 | (trade paperback)
Subjects: GSAFD: Ghost stories. | Horror fiction.
Classification: LCC PR9619.4.C628 W45 2021 | DDC 823/.92--dc23
LC record available at https://lccn.loc.gov/2020049756

Printed and bound in the United States of America.
VP 12 11 10 9 8

CHAPTER 1

KEIRA CRACKED HER EYES open. Rain fell through tree branches and pinged off her flushed skin, washing tracks of blood away from her cheek.

Footsteps crunched through leaves somewhere behind her, then faded into background noise. Keira pushed herself to sit up and swallowed a groan as pain radiated through her arm. She touched her shoulder, trying to find the source of the injury, but her jacket covered it.

Okay. So I'm in a forest, and I'm hurt. What happened?

She probed for memories but came up empty. Her name was Keira. She'd woken in a forest of some kind in the early evening, coated in mud, sore, and soaking wet. That was the extent of her knowledge.

Keira raised her hands. They seemed vaguely familiar, almost like an outdated photograph of someone she knew, but did nothing to cut through the fog.

A gunshot boomed from somewhere to her right. It was followed by a beat of silence, then a voice called a command in a language she didn't know.

Keira stiffened. The voice wasn't familiar, but its tone caused her pulse to spike and filled her mouth with the bitter tang of fear. *Run*, her subconscious urged her. *Run far and fast and quiet. You're being hunted.*

She was on her feet in a fraction of a second. Her head throbbed and her limbs shook as she staggered to a tree for support. *I can't have been out for long. A few seconds at most. I feel like I just finished running a marathon and my prize was getting hit by a train.*

She blinked rain out of her eyes as she tried to get her bearings. She'd woken in a small hollow between two trees. A muddy track ran down one side of the slope, apparently marking the place where she'd fallen.

The gunshot had come from her right. The rain had muffled the sound, which meant it must have been at least fifty meters away. That seemed like a lot of space and, at the same time, hardly any at all.

Keira moved in the opposite direction. Her lungs ached and a coppery film coated her tongue, but her legs seemed to know what to do. They moved quickly and lightly, carrying her over fallen branches and around holes. Her torso bent low, to make her a smaller target. Evidently, evading strangers had entered muscle memory.

The trees thinned ahead, and Keira put extra length into her strides. Despite her exhaustion, her body moved through the forest's edge and down the weed-choked slope with animalistic agility. It would have been exhilarating if she hadn't felt so disoriented.

Thick rain poured over her. She was in a thunderstorm, a proper, thorough one, the kind that only came a few times a year and was heavy enough to fill her mouth when she tilted her head back. *Good*, her mind whispered. *It will mask your scent and hide your tracks. They won't be able to use their dogs.*

She tried to hold on to that thought, sensing that the mystery of her existence would become clear if she could only follow it, but then it slid back into her subconscious like a phantom eel.

A foggy clearing stretched ahead of her. Beyond that was a town where distant, rain-blurred lights promised sanctuary.

The gun cracked again. Keira automatically bent lower, moving almost parallel to the ground, and switched her trajectory toward the closest building. It appeared to be some kind of farmstead set apart from the town, and golden light poured from its windows.

The ground leveled out, making Keira work slightly harder for each stride, and the grass grew high around her boots. Fine, chilled mist swirled in the rain.

A dark shape appeared through the fog, and Keira skidded to one side to avoid it. It was tall—almost as tall as she was—and seemed to be made of stone. She wanted to stop and take a closer look, but it felt like a bad time to inspect the scenery.

Lightning cracked through the sky and bathed the world in momentary white. Another shape appeared to her right. She squinted at it as she passed, and a chill ran along her spine. It was a gravestone. She'd stumbled into a cemetery.

More and more stones appeared around her, materializing out of the mist like ships sailing through ethereal waters. The building, which she'd mistaken for a farmstead, resolved itself into a small parsonage. A cross jutted from its steeple, dripping water onto the dark roof below.

The stone house looked at least a century old, but its garden was full of wild shrubs. As she drew along its side, Keira caught strains of music floating through the air.

She pressed herself to the building's side, where the shadows would disguise her, and looked back. The forest's edge was barely visible through the mist. Dark figures were slinking out of the tree line. At least a dozen of them.

Keira pressed a hand to her chest and felt her heart pounding. It had taken her less than a minute to reach the parsonage; she didn't think the men following her would be much slower.

"Please let me in." She whispered the words as she beat her fist against the wooden door. "Please, please, please."

The music fell silent. Keira pressed close to the stone, trying to hide inside the alcove, as she listened to footsteps move through the building. There was the muted click of a handle turning, and the door swung open to reveal a white-haired, spectacled man.

He carried an embroidered tea towel in one hand, and a threadbare maroon sweater covered gently slanted shoulders. His bushy eyebrows rose, a mixture of curiosity and bewilderment.

"Please, let me in." She threw a glance over her shoulder. They couldn't be far away; she likely only had seconds. "Someone's following me. Just let me hide here until they're gone, then I'll leave, I promise."

"Oh." He said the word very slowly as his eyes skipped from her drenched form to the trickle of blood running down her face. He blinked, then he nodded, as though he'd deemed her proposal reasonable enough, and stepped aside. "In that case, I suppose you had better come in."

She slipped through the doorway and pressed close to the wall. Her heart was thundering and her ears ringing. She could only hope she'd been fast enough that the strangers hadn't seen her.

The entryway was warm and smelled like spices, and the jumble of mismatched furniture clustered against its walls felt homey. The pastor closed the door, then put his back to it, watching Keira with faint bemusement. "What happened, child? Were you attacked?"

Keira licked rainwater off her lips. A part of her wanted to stay silent. She only needed to hide in the clergyman's house until the strangers lost her trail, and caution suggested she reveal as little about herself as possible.

On the other hand, she owed the pastor for his hospitality. The least she could do was answer his question. And maybe she'd unburden her own mind a little in the process.

"My name's Keira. I'm being hunted. That's all I can remember." She glanced along the hallway. Lamps were spaced around the old, scratched tables, their bulbs creating a mesh of conflicting light sources. Outside, thunder crackled. "Sorry, do you mind me asking...where am I?"

"Blighty Parish, two kilometers from the eponymous Blighty." He reached out to take her arm, but Keira moved away from the touch. The pastor didn't comment as he tactfully redirected the motion into a gesture toward an open door to their right. "Come and sit by the fire. You must be freezing."

She never had the chance to respond. The door boomed, shuddering as a heavy fist beat at its exterior. Something like electricity rushed through Keira, setting her brain buzzing and turning her fingers numb. *Hide*, her mind whispered. *Hide, or you won't be the only one to suffer.*

The pastor glanced at the door and lowered his voice. "Is that them?"

Keira could only nod.

The pastor's lips pursed. He crossed to a large, heavy wood wardrobe and opened the door. *In here*, he mouthed, beckoning to her.

Keira gratefully slipped among the assortment of patched coats, umbrellas, and rain boots. The fist returned to the door, louder, and the pastor closed the wardrobe on her.

"I'm coming, don't worry." His voice had been steady when he'd spoken to her, but now it took on a warbling, feeble note as he called out to his new visitors. "These old bones don't move as fast as they used to, bless me."

She listened to him approach the front door, each step an exaggerated shuffle. The door groaned as he opened it and the sound of drumming rain intensified. With it came a new, unpleasantly raw noise. *Heavy breathing*, Keira thought. *They've been running and are trying not to show it.*

"Good evening."

The voice sent a spasm of repulsion through Keira's stomach. The speaker was trying to sound respectful, but she could almost taste the frustration concealed in it. "I'm looking for my friend. A young woman, thin, with light-brown hair and wearing dark clothes. Have you seen her?"

"Well, now…" The pastor hesitated, and Keira tasted fear. "I saw a young woman of that description in town earlier this week. You're testing my memory, bless you, but I think she was—"

"No, tonight." The voice became harsh as it cut across the pastor's ramble, and the stranger cleared his throat before continuing in a calmer tone. "We became separated less than an hour ago." A pause, then he added, "We had a small disagreement. She might have asked you to keep her presence a secret. But the sooner we can be reunited, the sooner I can help her."

"Ah, forgive me, child. I haven't seen anyone between coming home this afternoon and opening my door a moment ago."

Thank you, Keira thought, clenching her fists to keep the fingers from shaking.

"Are you certain?" A hint of warning was introduced to the words. "It's very important that I find her."

"Bless you. Lying is a sin. I hope you don't think I'd endanger my immortal soul over something so trivial."

There was a silence that Keira struggled to interpret. She held her shoulders pressed tightly against the wardrobe's back, fighting to keep still and not betray her presence. The rain seemed deafening. Keira had the awful sense that the stranger wasn't going to be turned away so easily.

"On that subject," the pastor's voice took on tones of rapture, "I can't help but feel that some greater purpose has led you to my home on this black night. Would you come in for a few moments? We could discuss your soul's blessed destination over a nice cup of tea."

The stranger didn't bother trying to smother a disgusted grunt. Heavy feet crunched over the gravel path as he backed away. "Perhaps another time. I need to keep looking for my friend."

"Safe journey, child," the pastor called. A moment later, the front door groaned closed, and Keira dared to breathe again.

"Well. What fun." The feeble tone dropped from the pastor's voice as he opened the wardrobe, making Keira blink against the sudden light. "Whether it's solicitors, tax men, or nosy relatives, I've never had that line fail on me. Come on, Keira, you're getting water all over my shoes."

CHAPTER 2

"YES, SIT THERE, PLEASE," the pastor said. "I don't like that one, so I won't mind if it gets water stained."

Keira obediently sank into the paisley armchair. The parsonage's cozy sitting room was filled with an odd assortment of furniture, both modern and antique. A large fire crackled in the grate, radiating warmth through her soaked jeans and T-shirt, reducing some of her chills. The pastor took Keira's jacket, hung it next to the hearth to dry, then turned to a door on the other side of the room. "My name's John Adage, but I'm generally called just Adage. I think I have a first aid kit somewhere. Sit still a moment."

"Thank you," Keira called after his retreating back. She'd already said it when he let her out of the wardrobe, but once didn't seem like enough. "And, um, sorry for making you lie."

"Oh, don't worry about *that*." The clatter of plates told Keira her rescuer was in the kitchen. "Even ignoring the fact that betrayal would be a far greater sin, I never actually said anything untruthful, only that I hadn't seen anyone between coming home and opening the door."

Adage appeared in the doorway, a steaming bowl in one hand and a small white box in the other. He put the bowl into Keira's hands, and she discovered the source of the tasty spice smell that permeated the house. It was some kind of stew, and Keira realized she was ravenous. She scooped a spoonful into her mouth, swallowed as quickly as the hot liquid would allow, and went back for more.

"You're lucky you came tonight." Adage pulled a wooden chair up beside her and opened the white box. "I usually only cook stew once a week. If you'd come yesterday, I would have been serving you TV dinners instead."

Keira froze, spoon halfway to her mouth. "I didn't mean to take your food—"

"Don't be ridiculous." He pushed his glasses farther up his nose as he squinted at the instructions on the back of a bottle of antiseptic. "My job description includes feeding the poor, but there's hardly anyone poor enough in this town to feed. You'll do in a pinch."

Keira couldn't stop her laughter. She felt ludicrous. How the pastor could be so complacently cheerful was beyond her.

"Here we go." He shook a cotton ball out of its bag and poured some of the clear liquid onto it. "This will probably hurt. Medical things always do, in my experience. That man wasn't telling the truth, was he?"

Keira tried not to flinch as he pressed the cotton ball to her skin just below her hairline. "No. I don't think so anyway. I don't remember anything."

"Amnesia?"

"I suppose so."

"Hmm." He dabbed a few times, then threw the cotton ball into the fire and began hunting for bandages. "Well, I've never met you before, which means you're not from Blighty. It's a tiny town, too small to avoid an acquaintance with anyone, which can sometimes be as much a curse as a blessing. You could be from Broadmeadow. It's a twenty-minute drive away."

Keira shrugged. "The name doesn't ring any bells."

Adage frowned as he began unraveling a roll of bandages. "I have no idea what I'm doing here, I'm afraid. Perhaps I should call the doctor."

"No, you're doing great." The words tumbled out of her unbidden. The impulsive, reflexive part of her was certain she wanted to avoid hospitals and anything associated with them. "It doesn't even hurt anymore. Just put a bandage on it, and it'll be fine."

"Mm." Adage didn't sound convinced, but he leaned forward to wrap the cloth around her head. "I can't say I'm disappointed. Dr. Kelsey is a bit of a... Well, we're told to love our enemies, in which case I can safely say that I love no one more than Dr. Kelsey." He finished wrapping the bandage like a bandanna. "How does that feel?"

"It's great." It was growing soggy from her wet hair and felt loose, but Keira wasn't about to complain.

"Then I suppose we'd better figure out what we're going to do with you." Adage closed the first aid kit and nudged the bowl in Keira's hands, encouraging her to continue eating. "Do you have any memories at all? A surname or a friend's name, perhaps?"

Keira probed her mind. She made it as far back as waking up in the clearing, but everything beyond that was blank. *C'mon, brain. You have one job.* "Sorry."

He shrugged as though the situation were no more complicated than choosing what to order for dinner. "In that case, you can spend the night here if you promise not to steal anything or murder me in my sleep. We'll make you up a bed on one of the couches. Tomorrow, if you still can't remember, I'll ask around town."

Keira looked from the bowl of stew at the warm fire, then at the pastor. Simple thanks seemed wholly inadequate in return for the unquestioning generosity he'd shown her, but it was all she had to offer. "Thank you so much."

He waved away the gratitude as he crossed the room. "Really, tonight has become quite thrilling. It's a nice change from the usual pace. Let me have a look for some spare blankets."

Thunder cracked outside. The night was dark, but faint lights from the town created a mosaic on the wet glass. Anxiety tightened in her chest.

She had no actual memories of her life, but her subconscious kept feeding her tiny clues. *Rain is good,* it said. *It will wash away your footprints. Being found is bad; you don't want to know what those men are capable of.*

She turned back to the pastor, who was hunting through a

wardrobe and muttering as dead moths fell out from between the blankets. *If they find me here, they'll kill him.*

Her appetite vanished and she dropped the spoon back into the bowl. Adage had shown her more kindness than she could have hoped for; she would never forgive herself if he were hurt— or worse—because of it. "Uh, do you have somewhere else I could stay? A barn or something a bit more remote?"

He looked over his shoulder and raised his eyebrows questioningly.

"Those men might come back. I'd feel safer if I was somewhere better hidden." It was as close to the truth as she could get without letting him guess how dark her thoughts had become. He seemed to buy it, though, and pursed his lips in thought.

"The church has awful insulation. You'll freeze to death if I put you there… Oh, I know. We have a groundskeeper's cottage behind the graveyard. It's been empty since Peterson passed on last year, bless him, but it has a bed and a fireplace, and there shouldn't be more than the normal amount of rats. Would that do?"

Keira dearly wanted to know how many a "normal amount" of rats entailed, but she wasn't in a position to be choosy. "Sounds perfect!"

"Finish your stew, then, and I'll take you to it."

Keira shoveled the warm stew into her mouth while Adage went back into the kitchen. She could hear him digging through drawers, and he returned holding a large, rusty ring with a single key hanging from it.

"Ready." Keira put the bowl aside and snagged her still-wet

jacket off the chair. The idea that her presence might be a threat to the older man had embedded itself. Something in her stomach said that the strange men would search the area quickly, and they wouldn't give up easily.

Adage led her back to the hallway wardrobe and pulled out a pair of heavy coats and two umbrellas. "People leave them at the church," he explained as he handed one of each to Keira. "I usually keep them until they're claimed, but these have been waiting for their owners for the better part of a year, so I think it's safe to borrow them. Ready?"

Keira felt a little ridiculous pulling the raincoat over her already-wet clothes, but she did so anyway. "Ready."

The parsonage's thick walls had done a good job of blocking out noise, but the storm's intensity assaulted them as soon as the door was open. A heavy sheet of rain came across the threshold, buffeting them and making a mockery of their supposedly water-proof coats. Keira scanned the surrounding area as she waited for her companion to close the door. She looked for motion or for hulking, watching shapes, but the deluge made it impossible to see more than a dozen meters.

"This way." Adage had to bellow to be heard through the rain.

Keira followed in his shadow, careful not to let the distance between them grow too great for fear of losing him. The spongy ground sucked at her boots, and the wind made them both stagger as they trudged across the field to reenter the graveyard she'd passed through less than an hour before. The gravestones, dark from rain, loomed out of thin mist. It seemed disorganized, an assortment of traditional headstones battling for space around elaborate sculptures of angels and tall, cowled figures. Keira couldn't stop herself from staring at each passing face, searching for awareness in their eyes or a twitch of motion in their hands. The fog twisted and swirled about the grave markers, dancing in the rain. Chills ran over Keira as fingerlike tendrils brushed her cheeks.

"Just up ahead," the pastor called, and Keira saw a small building near the edge of the forest. She thought she must have passed close to it when dashing to the parsonage.

The cottage didn't seem large enough to hold more than two or three rooms. Dark, uneven slats covered a sharply peaked roof, and vines grew up one wall. The windows were cold and empty, and an atmosphere of neglect surrounded the hut. It struck Keira as a lonely building, hidden as far from civilization as possible, with a forest on one side and a garden of graves on the other.

Adage huddled close to the door as he fit the key into the lock and struggled to twist it. The door ground on its hinges as it opened, and they both shuffled into the relative comfort of a dry room.

"Like I said, an exciting night." Adage closed the door and shed his coat. Keira couldn't help but feel impressed that he'd maintained the note of warm optimism. "Let's see…it should still have power… Ah."

He'd found the switch, and golden light filled the space. Keira shrugged out of her coat as she stared around the cottage. Instead of dividing the tiny building into even tinier rooms, the bedroom, kitchen, dining, and lounge areas had all been combined. A door at the back led to what she guessed was a bathroom, but otherwise, the entire house was just one room.

She could have crossed the space in ten paces, but it had a comfortable, welcoming atmosphere. The single bed wedged against the left wall was covered in a colorful patchwork quilt, and a small kitchen offered the comfort of a kettle and stovetop.

"We'll get a fire going so that you don't freeze to death," Adage said, weaving around the overstuffed lounge chair to reach the dark hearth. "There's no heater, I'm afraid, but there should still be some spare blankets in the cupboard over there if you need them."

"I'll be okay from here." Keira followed the pastor to the fire and eased the kindling bucket out of his hands. She was dripping on the large rug that took up the center of the room, so she shuffled back onto the wooden boards. "Thank you so much. For everything."

"I'll help you settle in," he said happily. "I don't mind, really."

Keira managed a tight laugh. "Actually, I was really hoping to get out of these wet clothes…"

It was a half-truth. She was shivering, but her more urgent worry was making sure the strange men didn't discover the pastor's deception. If Adage left quickly, the storm would still be strong enough to wash away his footprints, but she didn't know how much longer the deluge would last.

"Oh! Oh, of course. I'll leave you to it, then." Adage picked his coat off the hook beside the door and shook off some of the excess water. "You know where to find me if you need anything. And tomorrow, I'll see if I can uncover any leads in town. Have a good sleep, Keira."

"Thank you, Father."

"Wrong religion," he said cheerfully, then let himself out. A torrent of rain poured through the doorway, seeming to embrace the pastor as he closed the door behind himself.

Keira crossed to the window and pressed against the chilled glass as she watched her new, unexpected friend march into the graveyard. Clumps of fog clung to his hunched form, looking almost like wraiths grasping at his coat. He disappeared into the night within five paces.

At least he'll be safe now... I hope.

Alone, Keira couldn't ignore how quiet the cottage was. Rain still beat against the roof, and the wooden supports groaned under the strain, but inside felt strangely isolated from the storm.

Keira stepped back from the window and looked at her hands. Just like in the forest, they seemed both very familiar and completely unrecognizable. She took a deep breath and clenched them into fists. "Okay. Time to figure out who the hell you are, Keira."

CHAPTER 3

KEIRA WAS FREEZING AND soaked, but she ignored the fireplace in favor of searching for a mirror. She figured she had at least an hour before hypothermia set in, and her missing identity was digging at her like an itch she couldn't reach.

As she'd guessed, the door at the back of the room led into a bathroom-slash-laundry. She turned on the light and found a bedraggled, wide-eyed stranger staring back at her through the sink's mirror.

So, this is what I look like. She stepped closer to the reflection and pulled the limp crown of bandages out of her hair. *It's not what I expected.*

After running through the forest so swiftly and efficiently, she'd imagined having a toned, fit body, the sort of figure that comes from drinking wheatgrass smoothies for breakfast and having memberships for three separate gyms. Instead of a twelve-pack and a Marine Corps tattoo on her bicep, the person looking back at her was bone-thin, with a pale face and too-large eyes.

Keira lifted her T-shirt's hem. There were no abs underneath and not a hint of fat either. Her ribs jutted out under anemic skin. She looked as though she'd either been starved or…

She pointed a warning finger at her reflection. "So help me, Keira, you'd better not be addicted to anything illegal. Because I know exactly zero drug dealers, and I'd really prefer not to go through withdrawal on top of everything else."

Her face, which she'd initially thought was meek and mousy, took on some personality as she spoke. That was good; she might have a chance of being taken seriously after all.

"No wonder Adage was so willing to help you," she grumbled as she began peeling off the wet clothes. "You look like an orphan waif straight out of a Hollywood movie. Please, sir, can I have some more porridge?"

Her jeans were hard to get off and tripped her when she tried to pull them over her feet. She bumped into the wall and hissed as pain flashed through her arm.

I forgot I was hurt there too. She twisted to see a long, straight cut not far below her shoulder. *Keira, you're a mess. How many terrible life choices did you make to end up like this?*

The skin around the cut looked red, but it wasn't bleeding, so she decided it could wait until later.

She didn't like the idea of walking around a stranger's house naked, so Keira left her underwear on. The cupboard in the bathroom's corner held spare blankets, so she took one, wrapped it around herself like a coat, and carried the wet clothes back to the main room.

The storm created a steady drone on the cottage's shingle roof as Keira built her fire. In the same way her legs had known how to run, her hands seemed to hold on to the memory of how to light the kindling, and the blaze was soon radiating heat through the room.

Keira stayed kneeling in front of it for a minute, hands extended, as she absorbed some of the warmth. Once her shaking stopped, she plucked the pile of wet clothes off the hearth and shook them out.

The T-shirt seemed cheap and well worn; she guessed it had been teal before repeated washing bled the color down to a watery gray. The jeans had a rip in the side, and not the deliberate, fashionable kind. But the boots and jacket both seemed to be of good quality, although old. She supposed that made sense; they were the two most valuable pieces of clothing for someone roughing it: sturdy shoes to protect her feet and a thick jacket to keep her warm. She hoped she hadn't stolen them.

After draping the T-shirt over the back of a wooden chair, she propped the boots in front of the fireplace to dry. Keira then felt through the pockets. The jeans were empty, so they joined the T-shirt to air out, but the jacket had two zippered nooks full of treasure. A crumpled twenty-dollar bill came out of the left pocket. And, in the right, she found a small black-and-white photograph.

Keira unfolded the picture carefully and squinted at the grainy figures. It depicted three people, two men and one woman, facing the camera. They all wore neutral expressions and stiff, strange suits. The clothes looked like some kind of uniform, but Keira couldn't guess which sector they belonged to.

The first man—tall and with an exceptionally thin face—and the middle-aged woman with a pinched mouth and rectangular glasses prompted no emotional response. The third figure, though, made bile rise in the back of Keira's throat. She knew him. She hated him.

Why? C'mon, brain, throw me a bone here. What did he do to you? Is he a relative? No, you don't know him that well... A friend's parent? A boss? Some jerk who keyed your car?

She squinted at the face. It was deeply scored with creases, although he couldn't have been more than forty. Heavy brows complemented a thick jaw and dark hair. The eyes held an unnerving intensity even when screened by the camera. A silvery shape over the lapel of his suit was faintly reminiscent of a name badge but was too small to see clearly. She sensed that it was some kind of insignia, like a medal or military rank, that set him apart from his peers.

She flipped the photo over. Someone had penciled seven words onto the back. Keira scrunched her mouth as she read them.

DON'T TRUST THE MEN WITH FLAKY SKIN

"Okay." She tilted her head to the side as though that might somehow make the message clearer. "So should I stay away from people with dandruff or what?"

Unsurprisingly, the message didn't reply. Keira carefully placed the photo on top of the fireplace mantel, where it could dry out, then dragged the couch closer to the hearth and snuggled into it.

Searching her clothes had given the fire time to warm her. She pulled her feet up under her and folded the blanket around herself as she watched the flickering flames.

I've been lucky, she thought as thunder cracked overhead. *Sure, the whole no memory thing sucks pretty badly, but in other ways, I couldn't have had better fortune. Tonight could have been spent hiding in an alley or huddled in the forest. Instead, I've been given food, shelter, and the promise of help. That's a lot to be grateful for.*

And hey…maybe it's a good thing I don't know who I was before. Some part of my life must have gone very wrong for me to end up like this. Maybe this is the universe's way of giving me a second chance.

She turned to watch the rain flow down the window. Mist coalesced just beyond the glass, seeming to caress the frame as it passed.

Keira frowned. She could have sworn she'd heard something. A deep wailing sound, distorted and muffled by the fog until it was close to inaudible. She waited, holding her breath. The mist beyond the window seemed to thicken. It was like a soup, swallowing the cottage, cutting her off from the rest of the world.

The noise came again. A woman howling deep, wretched cries.

Keira rose, her bare toes curling lightly as she paced across the dusty wood floor. She approached the nearest window: a pane divided into six squares, overlooking the cottage's dead front garden and, beyond that, the graveyard.

The noises had sounded close, like they might be coming from the cemetery itself, but at the same time, they'd been heavily muffled, as though Keira were wearing earplugs. Only the faintest strains of sound came through.

Her breath formed a cloud of condensation on the glass. The night was too dark and too wet to think that anyone would have come to mourn at the gravestones, but Keira couldn't stop herself from searching the dark monuments. They were disturbing; some were as tall as a human, many had tilted, many others grew lichen and robes of moss. In the smothering fog, their irregular outlines almost looked like sentries surrounding Keira, motionless as they stared at her.

One shifted. Keira's heart caught in her throat. Her eyes burned as she stared toward the space where she was certain a gravestone had existed seconds ago. It was now just empty space, filled by tendrils of mist.

It's not the men. No. This is something else.

The wailing noise teased at the edges of her hearing. It was deep and low, and although it was growing quieter, Keira thought it was also moving nearer.

The sudden urge to barricade her windows and lock the doors took hold of her. She reached for the curtains and gripped a fistful of musty fabric in each hand but still hesitated. The moving fog and sentry gravestones played tricks on her eyes. She thought she heard dead leaves crunch somewhere to her left, but it could have just been the effects of the rain.

The sounds of wailing had blended so thoroughly into the

droning rain that they caught Keira off guard when they stopped. The sound strangled out mid-howl, killed as thoroughly as though someone had clamped a hand over the victim's mouth.

Keira waited, her breathing shallow, hands still gripping the curtains, fearful but reluctant to block out her view of the surrounding land.

A woman's hand reached past the window frame. It came from Keira's left, the owner's body hidden by the stone wall. Twitching fingers felt along the metal joining the glass panes. Ragged fingernails tapped the glass.

Keira smothered a gasp and lurched back. The curtain rods rattled as she belatedly let go of the fabric, and the curtains swung on either side of the view they framed. The hand retreated back out of sight.

Something had been very wrong about the hand. Shock rooted Keira to the spot, and it took a second for her to register what she'd seen.

She'd been able to look *through* the skin. Even as the hand had pressed against the glass, scrabbling along the panes, she'd still been able to see the twisting fog and black monuments behind it.

No. Not possible.

She swallowed and edged to the side, trying to see around the wall that blocked her view of the unwelcome presence. Something flickered on the edge of her vision. Something translucent: a layer of pale white blending into the mist, barely highlighted by the glow flowing out from her cottage's windows. Keira took a step closer, craning her neck, trying to see the shape more clearly.

Two dead eyes stared at her from behind curtains of flowing hair. The specter moved forward, closing the distance between them, and Keira scrambled back. The ethereal form dissolved into the rain as easily as a breath of warm air on a cold night.

Keira's back hit the chair she'd rested on. She clutched for it, digging her fingers into the soft fabric, as her mind scrambled. The figure was gone, but she still wasn't alone. At the edges of her hearing were the heavily distorted wails.

What was *that?*

The answer came quickly. *Ghost.*

Sticky fear filled Keira's mouth. That answer had come from her subconscious—and it had come easily. Whoever she had been before her memories were wiped, she'd not only believed in ghosts but knew them well.

"Normal people don't see ghosts. Normal people probably don't even *believe* in ghosts." Keira held still, pressed close to the chair as her heart thundered. Her eyes darted between the windows, waiting for the woman to reappear. The fire no longer felt warm on her skin.

Can she get inside? The idea sickened Keira. Closely followed on its heels was a more unpleasant question: *Can she hurt me?*

Her subconscious remained silent, but she had the unpleasant sense that the answer was yes to both. Mist continued to swirl outside, but there was no sign of the woman. Slowly, cautiously, Keira approached the window again. She reflexively rolled her bare feet as she walked, minimizing any noise she might make on the wooden floorboards.

The storm was fading as the clouds' load diminished, but the drizzle was still thick enough to block most of the outside world from her view. She could see faraway lights from the parsonage and, even farther beyond that and barely visible, the distant town's lights. The rain-slicked tombstones protruded from the ground like rotten, crumbling teeth.

The ghost came out of nowhere, long fingers splayed as they pressed against the window. Keira flinched backward. If the glass hadn't divided them, she was certain she would have felt the specter's frozen breath on her skin.

Keira stopped an arm's length from the window. She and the ghost stared at each other, neither willing to break eye contact, neither moving. The woman was close to indistinguishable from her surroundings; if Keira let her vision blur, the figure faded into the background. But when she strained, she could make out a myriad of details.

The woman wore an old-fashioned sundress with a high neckline. Although the ghost held no color, the sunflower pattern made Keira think the dress might have been yellow in life, and it looked as though it could have belonged to the seventies or eighties. Her long hair hung limply around her shoulders but was dry in spite of the rain. The drops, wholly indifferent to the ghost's existence, passed through her.

The woman's eyes had no pupils, iris, or whites but were completely black. *Dead eyes*, Keira thought again, and she took a slow, cautious step forward. The woman mimicked the motion, leaning toward to the glass. Keira didn't know if the apparition could move through the walls, but the hand resting against the windowpane did nothing to interrupt the water droplets rolling down the surface.

A dark substance drenched the left half of the figure's face and stained the sundress, contrasting with the summery floral pattern. It came from a hole at her temple. When she focused on the area, Keira could make out tiny bone fragments jutting from the injury.

She was murdered. Is that why she didn't pass on?

The spirit's lips moved. She was speaking, but Keira couldn't hear the words. Against her better judgment, she stepped up to the window and angled her ear toward the glass.

She could hear the low reverberation of falling water and even catch individual pings as larger drops hit the window, but the ghost was either inaudible or too soft to hear through the storm.

Keira moved back and clutched the blanket a little tighter around herself. "I can't hear you. I'm sorry."

The woman's face contorted. She was still speaking, forming the same phrase over and over with bloodstained lips. Her movements were slow and indistinct, but repeated so many times, Keira thought she could guess the phrase. *Help me.*

Uneasy, anxious nausea rose. She half wanted to call the pastor to come back—wasn't it his job to make sure souls reached the next life? But even with her botched memory, she knew it wasn't normal to see ghosts.

She licked her lips and leaned close to the window. "Do you need something?"

The spirit's long hair drifted around her head as she nodded. It was as though gravity couldn't properly touch her. She was speaking again, but the words came too quickly for Keira to have any hope of lip-reading them. The ghost motioned toward either the town or the parsonage—it was impossible to tell—then clasped her hands below her chin in supplication. She had begun to cry; tears ran down her cheeks, blending with the spilled blood, dripping into her mouth and off her chin. Her lips moved incessantly, the words inaudible but clearly desperate.

All Keira could do was shake her head. "I can't understand you."

The woman's features twisted in distress as she clutched at her head. Lightning cracked, flooding the scene with blinding light. Keira squinted, and when her vision cleared, she felt uneasy prickles rise through her. The space beyond the window was empty.

Thunder rumbled through the cottage, rattling its windows and making Keira hunch her shoulders. She peered through the mist, searching for her dead companion, but all that remained of the woman was a fading handprint on the outside of the glass.

CHAPTER 4

KEIRA ROLLED OVER AND groaned. She'd come to rest on her cut shoulder, and pain flared through the limb. She sat and pushed her hair away from her face. The couch, a double-seater, had been a disastrous choice for a bed. To be fair, though, she hadn't intended to fall asleep in it; the plan had been to spend the night awake and alert. But she'd been more tired than she'd thought and couldn't remember anything past the mantelpiece clock's gentle midnight chime.

Okay. Stock-taking time. How much do I remember?

She recalled the ghost, barely visible, pressing close to the window and silently begging for help. Adage's smile as he gave her stew. The men slinking from the woods as they searched for her. Waking up in the clearing. Nothing beyond.

"Did you delete your memory files or something?" she asked her brain. "Because this is starting to become really inconvenient."

The persistent amnesia was frustrating, but the early morning sunshine spilling through the windows almost made up for it. Keira, cheered by the sight, inhaled deeply and pulled the blanket around her body as she crossed to the window.

The outside world had transformed from a misty, indistinct maze into a surreal but beautiful landscape. A short stone fence ran along the perimeter of the cottage's neglected garden. Beyond its gateless opening was the cemetery. Greenery filled in gaps between mismatched grave markers: spindly shrubs, leafless trees, and clumps of weeds were dotted among the stones, providing relief from what might have otherwise been a stark scene. The graveyard stretched farther than Keira had first thought; more pillars peeked out from among the forest edge to her left.

Large puddles collected in dips or holes, and the shadowed side of the gravestones still looked wet. Mist clung to the scene, reluctant to be dispersed by the sun, and drifted in thin patches. Keira scanned the area for the specter she'd seen the night before—or any other unnatural figure—but the only person in sight was solid and human.

A man walked along a pathway leading into the cemetery. *Adage*, Keira thought, then caught herself. *No—that's not Adage, not unless he discovered the world's fastest-acting diet last night.*

She shrank back from the window so the room's shadows would hide her. The man was too far away to see his face clearly, but he was tall, clad in a thick coat, and carried something that looked like a briefcase as he moved with quick, purposeful steps.

Is it one of the men? She hadn't seen their faces the night before.

Don't jump to conclusions. This is a public cemetery. He might be coming to pay his respects to one of the graves.

Even so…

Keira crossed to the clothes she'd hung out to dry and began dressing with feverish urgency. She couldn't discount the idea that the man was there for her, and she did *not* want to go on the run in just underwear.

The clothes had an unpleasant stiff texture and were still damp about the seams, but she tugged them on, ignoring the way her shoulder stung when she flexed it. She hopped back to the window as she tied the second boot's laces.

The man was definitely coming to her cottage. He'd passed the last of the gravestones and was stepping over the puddles surrounding the cottage's fence.

Keira lowered herself out of sight, her heart thundering. The stranger had been fast, and there was zero chance of slipping through the door unseen. *Can I break a back window? Hide in the bathroom? Is it too late to lock the front door?*

Four sharp knocks echoed through the room. Keira hunched her shoulders further, silent.

"Hello?" The voice didn't sound aggressive at least, and Keira felt none of the visceral repulsion she'd experienced when hiding in Adage's wardrobe the night before. "Keira? Adage asked me to drop by. I'm…well, I'm technically not a doctor, but I spent the last few years in med school, and he wanted me to check in on you."

Keira began breathing freely again. "Coming!"

Her clothes were askew, so she straightened them, but there was nothing to do for the creases. She ran her fingers through her hair in a hopeless attempt to fix it as she crossed to let her visitor in.

The man had been looking over the graveyard but turned to face her as she opened the door. He was tall, and thick, dark-chocolate hair was casually pushed back from his forehead, but strands still fell down to brush near his green eyes. He smiled, and the expression warmed his whole face.

"Mason Corr," he said, extending his hand. "How are you feeling?"

"Remarkably okay, I think?" Instead of taking the offered hand, Keira stepped back, inviting him inside. "I just woke up, so I'm still taking stock, to be honest."

He had to dip his head slightly to get under the doorframe, but the smile didn't falter. "Sorry about that. I would have come at a more reasonable time, except Adage said you had a head injury and that's not really something you want to ignore."

"That's fair. There's, uh, seats and stuff if you want one." Keira grimaced, but Mason either didn't notice her awkwardness or tactfully ignored it.

He stopped in front of the wooden chair, put his briefcase on the ground, and patted the couch as an invitation for her to sit. "Adage also said you had some memory loss last night. How's that doing this morning?"

"Still…lossy." She shrugged as she sat. "I remember waking up in the forest. Nothing before."

"Do you remember everything after that?"

"Yes."

Mason nodded. "That's good. I'd be more worried if the loss was ongoing. Mind if I have a look?"

Keira obligingly bent forward and pointed to her hairline, where the skin still ached. Mason's fingers were unexpectedly warm and careful as he brushed her hair away from the mark.

"Odd," he murmured, so quietly that she guessed he must be talking to himself.

"What is it?"

His piercing green eyes glanced over her, and she knew he saw everything in that one swoop: the tear in her jeans, the way her wrist bones protruded, and the mud still caked over her boots. He made a small noise of discontent in the back of his throat and rose. "I've been a terrible guest. You said you'd just woken up; you probably want something to drink."

"Huh? No, I'm fine—"

Already at the kitchen, he threw her a smile over his shoulder. "Well, I'm getting myself something, so I may as well boil the kettle for two. What would you like? Tea? Coffee?"

His tone was nonchalant, but she couldn't shake the feeling that he was going to lengths to be nice to her. Keira followed him into the kitchen. "Let me make the drinks." She opened the closest cupboard, but it turned out to be full of dusty dishes.

A warm weight rested on her forearm, and she looked down to see his hand there. Mason gave a quick squeeze. "Don't worry about it. My dad and I used to visit Peterson, the old grounds-keeper, so I know my way around. Why don't you light the fire? It's a brisk morning."

Keira pulled away, her pulse unpleasantly fast, and crossed to the fireplace in two quick steps. She knelt, shoving fistfuls of kindling on top of the previous night's ash, and poked fire starters underneath it.

She didn't like being touched. She'd had the same reaction to Adage the night before when he'd tried to take her arm. And she thought she knew why. It had been a long time since she'd had any meaningful human contact. Possibly years.

She scrunched her mouth and glanced toward Mason. He was facing away, washing two mugs in the sink. Steam was already rising from the kettle's spout.

Keira dropped more wood onto the growing fire. Part of her wanted to finish the visit soon. Mason would probably leave if she said she wanted to sleep for a few more hours. But at the same time, the idea made her feel horribly alone. Surrounded by monuments to the dead, in a house that wasn't hers, she found she was grateful to have some company. Even if he'd only come as a favor to Adage.

"Keira?" Mason was standing by the counter, an old-fashioned tin raised in each hand, and rattled the containers. "Tea or coffee?"

"Uh…" She couldn't remember if she had a preference. He might as well have asked her if she liked her eggs to come from dragons or sea lizards. "Why don't you pick?"

Mason quirked his head. He was still smiling, but she sensed her answer concerned him. "Let's try the tea first, and we can switch to coffee if you don't like it. I didn't think to bring milk. Sorry."

"No problem."

He popped open the lid on one of the containers and turned back to the cups. "Can you have a think back for me, Keira? Do you remember anything from your life?"

"No." She'd already tried—multiple times. "Everything before last night is blank."

"Hmm." He dunked the tea bags several times then dropped them into the sink. Keira climbed onto her couch as he set the cup on the floor beside her. "I'll be honest with you. I don't know what to make of this. While complete memory loss isn't unheard of, it's not as common as the movies portray it. Usually, people only lose blocks of memories—a few minutes, a few months, a few decades—but can still recall earlier ones, especially from their childhood. The longer you've had a memory, the more solid it is."

"Ah." Keira pointed to her head. "And you don't think this is enough to cause complete memory loss?"

He scratched the back of his neck. "No, I don't. It's not an impact wound but a glancing blow—possibly from a knife or glass or similar. It cut the skin but doesn't look deep enough to cause any more significant damage."

That was a surprise—Keira had implicitly assumed the injury and the amnesia were linked.

Mason raised his hands in an open shrug. "Lots of things can cause memory loss. Even something like whiplash can be enough to interrupt the flow of memories from short term to long term. But like I said, complete loss isn't common. To lose everything, I would have expected to see severe cranial injuries."

Keira picked the mug off the floor to give herself something to do. Mason's tone hadn't been accusatory, but it was hard not to feel defensive. "I'm not making it up."

"Ah, no—that wasn't..." He looked genuinely embarrassed. "Sorry, I didn't mean to imply that. It's not what I was getting at. How our brains store memories is an incredibly complex process, and we still don't know how it works. Not really. We can guess and come up with theories, but the whole area is dotted with question marks."

"Can they come back?"

"Often, yes." Mason picked up his own drink, then leaned back in his chair and stared at the rising steam. "While there are some cases where the memories never return, most times, they do—either partially or completely. The brain is incredibly resilient. You might be able to help it re-form the connections by seeking out sights, sounds, smells, and tastes that might hold significance for your past life. Even just a small association—like your favorite drink—could be enough to bring something back."

Keira looked at her cup of tea. It was still hot, but she sniffed the liquid, then sipped it. Mason watched with raised eyebrows, and Keira couldn't stop a snorting laugh as she shook her head. "I think I like tea. But there's no angel chorus of returning memories."

His face warmed as he grinned. "Well, keep trying. It might take some time." The smile dropped, and he shifted forward. "But I should add, I'm not actually a doctor yet. I can give general advice, but I won't be anywhere near as helpful as a specialist.

Some scans and X-rays could give answers, too, especially as your case is so unusual. Blighty doesn't have a hospital, but I'd be glad to drive you to Cheltenham Medical."

A quiet, strangling panic moved through Keira. She kept her smile in place but could feel her knuckles turning white on the mug. *No hospitals. No doctors.* "Honestly, it's not so bad. I'll, uh…I'll see how I go over the next couple of days. It'll probably fix itself."

He tilted his head. The sharp green eyes flicked down to where her knuckles strained around the cup, then his smile was back in place. "Of course, it's completely up to you. Scans could rule out certain causes, but there's not much a hospital can do for treatment beyond therapy. You don't need to go if you'd prefer not to."

He must think I'm frightened of hospitals…which I guess is something close to the truth.

"Get lots of rest," he continued. "Eat nutritious food, especially good fats and leafy, green vegetables. Try to jog your memory, but don't push it. There's a decent chance your mind will re-form the connections over the next day or two."

"Thanks."

"The cut on your head is shallow; I don't think it needs stitches. Just keep it clean." He ran his fingers through his hair, ruffling it. "You're not hurt anywhere else?"

The mark on her arm had settled to a low, dull ache. Her first instinct was to tell Mason that she was fine and deal with the injury herself. *But*, logic argued, *Old Keira probably knew what to do to keep infection out. You don't.*

Her hesitation was enough to answer Mason's question. He placed his mug back on the floor. "What is it?"

"Just, uh, a cut on my shoulder."

"Let me see."

She shrugged out of the jacket, and Mason released a low hiss between his teeth. "This is nasty, Keira. You should have said something."

"It doesn't feel too bad."

He bent close, examining the cut without touching it. "It's almost to the bone. I can clean and stitch it, but honestly, you should see a proper doctor."

"No, thank you."

"I can drive—"

"Nope." She put a little more force behind the word.

Mason's lips tightened, but after a second, he nodded. "I don't have any anesthetic, so it'll hurt. Are you okay with that?"

One of the blessings of losing her memories was that she had very few experiences to make her wary of pain. "Bring it on."

Mason drew his chair closer, then lifted the case onto his lap. He flipped open the lid, revealing a mix of equipment and supplies that could have belonged in a hospital.

"I thought you weren't technically a doctor," she said as he tugged on a pair of gloves.

His grin was tight. "After about six months of training, my entire extended family decided that I was qualified enough to treat them for free. I've learned to be prepared."

She laughed, but her mirth was cut off when an

antiseptic-doused swap touched the exposed flesh. "*Ugh.* Could you poke it a little harder, please?"

"Sorry. I know it hurts." He looked appropriately contrite but continued dabbing at the cut.

Keira bit the inside of her cheek and turned toward the fire. She focused on the dancing flame, forcing her whole attention toward it in an attempt to push the pain into the back of her mind.

"You're turning out to be a very interesting person." Mason tossed aside one swab and fished out a new one. "The cut's clean. There aren't any jagged edges or tears—just a straight slice through."

"Yeah? What does that mean?"

He arched an eyebrow as he worked. "It rules out a lot of accidental injuries. I'm guessing this was made by either a large shard of glass or a knife. And…it was probably deliberate." His green eyes flashed up to gauge her reaction.

She grimaced. "So by process of elimination, I'm probably either a drug lord or a professional assassin."

His shoulders shook as he tried not to laugh. "Probably." After discarding the second swab, Mason tore open a little plastic pack that held a needle. "We're nearly there."

Keira squeezed her eyes closed as the needle cut into her and the thread drew her skin back together. It hurt less than the antiseptic had, but she didn't want to see her arm being turned into a craft project.

"Keira?"

"Hmm?"

Mason seemed to be speaking carefully. "I hope it's not rude to ask, but do you have food?"

"Oh, yeah, I'm fine." The answer came out automatically. Keira suspected she'd given it hundreds of times before.

He narrowed his eyes at her, and she knew he'd looked through the cupboards while making tea.

"Well, I have money. I was planning to go into town a bit later. Buy some supplies."

He nodded, but the cautious tone lingered. "Enough money?"

"Plenty." *Twenty counts as plenty, right?*

Mason looked relieved. "Good. Make sure you eat well. You lost a lot of blood from this, and you'll need energy to make more. And don't be afraid of asking for help if money gets tight, okay?"

"I will," she lied happily. She knew Mason's offers came from concern, but her subconscious screamed at the idea of accepting charity. Even staying in Adage's cottage felt unnatural. *Well, I guess that's a good response. It means I probably wasn't a thief...or that I was the worst thief ever.*

Mason tied off the sutures and cut the thread. "There. These can come out in a few days. Does it feel okay?"

She flexed her arm. "Much better now that it's not flapping open all the time."

He made a face and dug a bottle out of his case. "Painkillers," he explained as he tipped two into a smaller empty bottle and handed it to her. "Take one now and another tonight before bed. I don't think you'll need more. You've got a pretty high pain threshold."

"Yeah?"

"Not a single scream. Count me impressed." He made to close the case, but hesitated. "You're not hurt anywhere else, are you?"

"Nope."

He raised an eyebrow.

She held up her hands reassuringly. "Promise."

"Good." The cheerful, warming smile was back, and he locked his case.

Keira expected him to get up and leave, but he stayed sitting. One hand came up to rub the back of his neck as his eyes flicked over her. She could feel his gaze touching on all of her vulnerabilities—the unkempt hair, the stitches just below her shoulder, the protruding bones—and desperately hunted for a distraction.

"More tea?" she asked.

"Thank you, I'm fine." He inclined his head to one side. "Keira?"

"Yeah?"

"Will you still be here tomorrow?"

That question didn't have a simple answer. Sitting by the cottage's fire, surrounded by well-loved furniture and sipping a hot drink, she'd easily forgotten how uncertain her future was. She took a moment to form her reply. "I...don't know. It depends on whether my memory comes back. And whether Adage invites me to stay another night."

"He will."

Keira thought she saw something in Mason's face, but it was gone before she could fully identify it.

He rose and returned his cup to the sink. "In that case, I'll come by tomorrow to check your arm."

"That would be nice." She was surprised to realize how much she meant it. "Thank you."

He extended his hand.

She shook it, and this time, it was easier not to squirm at the contact, even when he didn't immediately release it.

Mason's smile extended into his eyes. "Take care, Keira. I'll see you again soon."

CHAPTER 5

STARVE OR GET SHOT at? Keira pulled a face as she stared through the cottage window at the puddles dotting the grave-yard. *Starve…or get shot at?*

She'd showered once Mason was safely gone. The clothes still felt grimy, but at least her hair no longer looked like a home for small critters. Now, she only needed food.

Keira's gut instinct said the strange figures that had chased her wouldn't stay in the town now that it was daytime, but for all she knew, her gut was an appalling liar. Her brain argued that safety should be paramount, and that all it would take was one moment of lowered guard to get sniped. On the other hand, she was really, really hungry. She'd been standing at the window for close to an hour but hadn't seen anything more interesting than a small flock of birds fighting over a grub.

Keira blew a breath out, crossed to the fireplace mantel, and took both the twenty dollars and the photograph. She didn't know the picture's significance, but it must have been important to be the only nonpractical thing she'd brought with her. She slipped it into her jacket pocket, zipped it closed, then went back to the door.

Even if I don't go to town, I should at least check on Adage. He called Mason, which means he made it through the night alive and unharmed, but I should still say good morning. He might even be able to tell me if any of the men came back—or if it's normal to see ghosts in his graveyard.

Keira dug her thumbs into the bridge of her nose. There was too much to think about—too much to *worry* about—and her mind felt dangerously close to fracturing under the pressure.

She pushed the cottage's door open and recoiled at the gust of chilled air. Although the sun had looked bright and generous from her window, the trees blocked much of it from warming the ground, and plumes of condensation rose from Keira's mouth when she exhaled. She slipped through the opening, shut the door to preserve the warmth for her return, and marched toward the gravestones.

The mist still hadn't disappeared, and Keira was starting to believe it was a somewhat permanent fixture in the cemetery. A long, soot-colored stone wall marked the cemetery's end a hundred meters ahead of her. She glanced to her left, where the ancient markers mingled with twisting trees at the forest's edge. The sight made her uneasy. *Why don't they stop at the forest? It's got to be the cemetery's border, right?*

She stomped her feet to get the blood moving, passed through the open gateway, and turned to her right. The overgrown dirt path led through an arrangement of flowering bushes that divided the graves from the parsonage's gardens. She kept her pace quick and her eyes constantly moving, wary of both strangers and ethereal figures looming through the fog. Water-stained angels and grim cherubs watched her progress. She tried not to make eye contact with any of the stone figures as she crossed her arms and increased her speed.

Keira couldn't tell if she was imagining it, but the pastor's yard felt warmer than the cemetery. The grass was thicker and neatly cut, and she rolled her shoulders as she returned to the same door she'd beaten against the night before.

A piece of paper was attached to the wood with peeling sticky tape. Keira bent to read the damp note.

Dear Keira,

Thank you for not murdering me in my sleep last night. That was very polite of you.

I've gone to town to make inquiries. Your situation might require some subtlety to keep the news away from unfriendly ears, so I'll be discreet.

I asked a young gentleman named Mason Corr to visit you today. He is a medical student, and I'm pleased to say he has a much better bedside manner than our resident doctor. Best of all, he's free. He may be able to give some answers regarding your memory.

Let yourself in—the door is unlocked. There's leftover stew in the kitchen. I should be back early afternoon.

Kindly yours,

J. Adage

Keira tried the door. As promised, it opened without resistance. "Unbelievable," she muttered, closing the door again and taking down the note. "Are you *trying* to get robbed?"

Blighty had to be a very trusting town. Or perhaps Adage was just an exceptionally trusting person.

The offer of stew was tempting, but she couldn't stomach the idea of taking more of his food, especially not when she had money to buy her own. She didn't know how much a pastor earned, but judging by the secondhand furniture, it wasn't enough to hand out favors as freely as he seemed inclined to.

Keira slipped the note under the door, where casual passersby wouldn't see it, then turned toward the driveway leading down to the clustered houses and shops in the distance. She didn't want to admit how much the trip frightened her. *They're probably not going to hang around town if they're still looking for you*, she reasoned. *And besides, a gunman is hardly likely to shoot at you in broad daylight in front of witnesses.*

Unless they're crazy. And let's be honest, if one person wants to shoot another, there's a good chance at least one of them is somewhat crazy. Fingers crossed it's not me.

Keira walked as quickly as she could without breaking into a jog.

She'd hoped to get out from under the trees and absorb some of the sun, but vast oaks lined the drive. They were filled with birds she couldn't see, and the shrill chatter seemed to welcome the clear day.

The path meandered as it wove around a narrow stream and eventually turned toward town. Keira passed through a thick copse of saplings and found herself at the road, where a large, hand-painted sign nailed to a tree read BLIGHTY CHURCH & BLIGHTY CEMETERY.

The road continued to her right as it wound into the hills and worked its way toward the next town. To her left was Blighty's main street, bordered by shops and home businesses. Keira whistled as she gazed over them.

Blighty had a heavy emphasis on old-world charm. Most of the buildings were stone and had thatched or shingle roofs, with tall, paned windows, like something she would expect to find in a Dickens novel. The shops all had hand-painted signs hung above them, and messy fern baskets were suspended from the eaves. Keira half expected the road to be cobble and had to look down to make sure it was still asphalt. Ahead, a large fountain marked the intersection of two roads, and beyond that, groups of houses grew outward from the town center. Morning was creeping toward noon, and the streets held a smattering of shoppers. Keira joined the flow and tried to blend in.

The closest shop was a narrow florist, conveniently close to the graveyard. Passing it felt like walking through a cloud of pollen. Keira stretched to look through the window at the bouquets filling the store. A short, pince-nez-wearing woman stood behind the counter, cutting ribbons. She squinted at Keira, one eyebrow raised. Keira ducked her head and kept moving.

They'll just think I'm a tourist. A quaint town like this must have hundreds of sightseers come through each year.

Keira tried to keep her eyes moving over her environment without drawing attention to herself. She could feel the occasional curious glance cast her way, and it sent prickles crawling up her arms and made her palms sweat. She was starting to regret venturing into public so soon.

The town's general store occupied one of the corners that bordered the central fountain. The shop needed a new coat of paint, but the door jingled cheerfully as she opened it. Inside seemed dim after walking through the sunlight, and Keira blinked as her eyes adjusted.

The store wasn't especially large, but it was filled with a boggling jungle of products. Boxes were stacked up to the ceiling, and shelves were so full that some were nearly overflowing. Keira took one of the wire baskets waiting beside the door and let her feet lead her into the nearest aisle.

Twenty won't get me much, she realized as she read some of the prices. *Especially as I need more than just food.*

She wove through the maze until she found the personal hygiene section, then picked out the cheapest toothbrush and soap available. The shampoo was expensive, so Keira passed on it and returned to the food section while calculating how much she had left to spend. Her mouth filled with saliva as she saw a lasagna in the freezer. She made to open the door but hesitated.

Rice, her mind whispered. *Potatoes. High calorie and low cost.* The idea came from her subconscious, and Keira was hardly surprised. Of course Old Keira would be adept at shopping with pennies. Old Keira probably knew which were the best bushes to sleep under too. She allowed herself the indulgence of a dramatic, longing sigh, then turned away from the lasagna and went in search of the dry goods.

Her basket was heavy by the time she turned toward the checkout. It was simultaneously reassuring and frightening; the food should last her at least a couple of days, but there wouldn't be any more until she found a way to earn money.

I might have my memories by then. There was only one person ahead of her at the checkout, so Keira joined the queue and did her best to fade into the background. *Though I'm not sure how much good those memories will do. Adage might be able to help me find some unskilled job around town. I could garden or wash windows for a few dollars...*

When the woman ahead finished paying and took her shopping, Keira stepped forward. She kept her head down as she unloaded the bags of rice, hoping the assistant would let her complete the transaction without any small talk.

No such luck.

"You're new here." The phrase was said curiously, almost wonderingly, and Keira raised her eyes.

The lady behind the checkout looked completely at odds with the quaint town. Violently red lipstick and dark eyeliner made her features pop, and her cropped hair was almost unnaturally black. She looked young—about Keira's age—and her brown eyes were wide and sparkling. "What sort of ghastly bad luck landed you in Blighty?"

It was exactly the sort of conversation Keira had been trying to avoid. She managed a tight smile. "Just passing through."

"No you're not." The woman propped her forearms on the bag of rice and bent forward, examining Keira's face with far more interest than Keira appreciated. "This is *Blighty*. No one 'passes through.' It's not close to anywhere and doesn't bridge any other towns, and its only claim to fame is being a miserable hole where dreams go to die."

Keira was lost for words. She glanced toward the store's door, barely six paces away, then looked behind herself. A short queue had formed, but both parties were deliberately facing away, clearly not wanting to get roped into the discussion. She cleared her throat. "Uh…I think it's a nice town."

The sales assistant bent even closer, leaning so far over the counter that she managed to invade Keira's personal space. One hand came up to tap at her lower lip as she narrowed her eyes. "I saw a dead guy outside my bedroom window last night. Now you, the first stranger I've seen in months, are standing in my store barely twelve hours later. Don't expect me to believe that's a coincidence."

"What?" Keira stared at the assistant, then looked back at the other shoppers. They continued to ignore her. *Is this a joke? Is she crazy? Did she seriously see a dead person? Does it have anything to do with—*

The assistant's eyes took on a fanatical glint as she somehow managed to stretch another inch nearer. Her voice dropped to a stage whisper. "Give it to me straight. Are we part of a government experiment?"

This can't be happening. My life is already too complicated. I'm not getting paid enough to deal with…whatever this is.

"Okay, okay, I understand." The woman finally slid back behind her counter and raised both hands reassuringly, though the effect was ruined by a conspiratorial wink. "You don't want to be overheard. Tell you what, I'll buy you a coffee, and we can go over this somewhere a bit more private." She pointed to a faded white name tag stuck to her chest. "Zoe, by the way."

"What?" Keira managed again. She felt as though she'd walked into a Picasso painting, where life just didn't make as much sense as it should.

"Coffee. Now. I have some questions. You'll give me answers. C'mon." Zoe was already pulling off her apron.

Keira's brain was doing its best to catch up. She found it hard to believe Zoe had seen an actual dead person at her window the night before—but there *had* been a genuine ghost outside the groundskeeper's cottage. She wasn't in a position to discount anything or reject any potential help, no matter how bizarrely it was packaged. "All right, okay. Coffee. But I need to pay for this first."

"Yeah, yeah, sure." Zoe grabbed the basket and riffled through. Before Keira knew what was happening, the other woman was prying the twenty out of her hand and shoving a couple of coins into its place. "That'll be nineteen fifty-five. Thank you for shopping at Blighty General. Now c'mon. If we're fast, we can get in before the lunch rush."

"But—"

Zoe piled the bags back into the basket and shoved it behind the desk. "You can pick this up on your way back through. Oy, Lucas, take over for me."

"What?" A skinny teen standing in line startled at the sound of his name.

Zoe snagged the boy's collar and hauled him behind the counter. "Just cover for me for the next half hour, okay?"

His eyes bulged with dawning horror. "But I don't work here."

"You'll be fine! Just scan stuff and take people's money." Zoe caught Keira's sleeve and dragged her through the door. The sudden sunlight made Keira squint. She had all of half a second to inhale the brisk air, then the pressure on her arm was pulling her toward the intersection.

Zoe didn't even check that their path was clear before striding onto the road, forcing a car to swerve to avoid them. Keira had no choice but to follow at a quick trot. Zoe was a head shorter than her but could have entered the Olympics for competitive power walking. As they reached the curb, she shot Keira a huge smile that was equal parts manic excitement and zealous determination. Keira tried to smile back, but it came out as a grimace.

I think she might just be insane.

CHAPTER 6

THE CAFÉ OCCUPIED THE corner opposite the general store. Keira only had a second to read the bright-yellow wooden sign above the door—*Has Beans*—before Zoe jerked her inside. It was a welcoming sort of café, with big, squishy chairs spaced around the various nooks and a bookcase half-full of worn paperbacks near the window.

"Oh good, the corner's free," Zoe said. The café wasn't quite full, but a small crowd had gathered, and the chatter blended in with the whirr of a coffee grinder. "That's the best table. What d'you want? My treat."

"Uhh—" Keira squinted to read the smudged chalkboard above the counter. Zoe had offered coffee, but it would be all right to get something else, wouldn't it? Something with a lot of sugar and fat for energy. "Hot chocolate?"

"Oy, Marlene!" Zoe bellowed over the queue of patrons

waiting to order. A sallow woman behind the counter looked up. "Bring us a hot chocolate and a caramel latte, okay? And two of those disgusting, overpriced muffins. I'll pay you back later."

Marlene gave a thumbs-up. Zoe shooed Keira toward a four-seater table in the corner between the window and the bookcase, then pushed her into one of the couches. The constant manhandling was grating on Keira's nerves, but she purposefully kept her demeanor calm.

Play it casual. She can't prove I'm not a tourist. And if I can redirect the conversation to the thing she saw outside her window, she might forget to ask too many questions.

Zoe took the seat opposite and shuffled it as close to the table as it would go. "Okay, spill the beans. Who're you running from?"

"Running?" Keira laughed airily. "I'm sorry for getting your hopes up, but I'm honestly just passing through."

Zoe gave her an intense deadpan glare. "Cut the crap. Tourists don't buy a lifetime supply of rice and potatoes. And you could have been following the CIA's training manual for how to not draw attention to yourself. I didn't even see you until you were standing in front of my counter."

Damn. She's quick. Keira's smile faltered, but she fought to keep her voice light. "This is going to be a disappointment, but I really don't have any answers. You said something about a face outside your window?"

Zoe folded her arms on the table and leaned closer. It was a mirror of the pose she'd adopted in the store, and Keira had to sink back into the couch's cushions to preserve her personal space.

"C'mon," Zoe said, her eyes intense under lowered eyebrows. "I'm not a moron. You twitched when I asked who you were running from. Is it an ex? Your parents? Interpol?"

Keira didn't answer. Her heart thundered and her clenched palms were sweaty. She glanced toward the door. It was close. *I could run.*

"Hot chocolate," a flat voice said, and a large mug hit the table in front of Keira, making her jump. "Caramel latte. And two reasonably priced muffins that are in no way disgusting." Marlene, the sallow barista, dropped the food on the table, then tweaked Zoe's ear. "You're being weird again. Stop scaring my customers away."

Zoe glowered at the barista's retreating back. "I am *not* being weird."

You sure about that? Keira glanced at the door again. Running meant she would have to abandon her food at the general store.

"Hey, hey, I'm sorry." Zoe tilted to block Keira's view of the door. Her face had lost the fanatical glow, and an awkward, apologetic smile took its place. "I didn't mean to make you uncomfortable. Don't go."

"I don't like being accused of lying." The edges of Keira's voice wavered, but she managed to keep her tone even.

Zoe exhaled. "Sorry. I can get carried away when I'm excited. Is there any chance we could start this whole interaction fresh?"

After all that? Keira searched her companion's face, but the apology seemed sincere.

"I'm Zoe Turner." Zoe's wide smile was back in place, and she stretched a hand forward. "Nice to meet you…?"

Keira hesitated for a second, then swallowed. "Keira." She shook Zoe's hand for the briefest second possible, then drew back to pick up the hot chocolate. It smelled delicious, and she was hungry enough to swallow a scorching mouthful.

Zoe leaned back into her seat and picked up her own mug, though she made no move to drink it. "Look, I don't know your deal, but I might be able to help. I know Blighty like the back of my hand, and at least half its secrets too. Take this place. Has Beans is run by Myrtle Kennard. Her sister, Polly, owns the florist's down the road. Wanna know what she calls it? Two Bees. Get it? Has-been and to be. Isn't that just the worst set of puns you've ever heard?"

Keira couldn't stop a smile from cracking her expression. "Yeah, that's pretty bad."

"Well, get this. The two sisters opened their businesses twenty years ago with money they 'inherited' from a 'benevolent' and 'extremely wealthy uncle.'" Zoe made air quotes around the phrases. Lowering her voice to a whisper, she added, "Except the uncle never existed. I've been right through the family records—he's fictional."

"Yeah?"

"Yeah. But incidentally, Myrtle and Polly are near-perfect matches for the description of a bank-robbing duo from the eighties."

"You're kidding."

Zoe lifted her shoulders in a carefree shrug. "I can't prove anything. And I wouldn't want to if I could. Myrtle and Polly are nice people. And the bank robbers never held hostages or did shoot-outs or anything; they just passed a note over the counter demanding money, took the cash, and ran. They hit eight banks over a three-month period, then disappeared about two months before the sisters moved to Blighty."

Keira glanced back at the counter, where Marlene was somehow pouring three coffees at once. *That's too crazy to be real. Isn't it?*

"Anyway, my point is, I can keep a secret. If you want to tell me what's happened, I can maybe even help."

Keira couldn't smother a laugh. "You just *shared* a secret. I can't say it's done much to build my trust in your restraint."

"Ah, but think about the hundreds of secrets I *haven't* told you!" Zoe winked. "Yet."

She's ridiculous. Against her better judgment, Keira was starting to warm toward the strange, energetic woman. Taking a long drink of her chocolate, she considered how much she should share and decided on the safest option. "You said you saw something outside your window. Tell me about that first."

"Fair enough." Zoe shoved both muffins toward Keira. "Eat. You look like Skeletor and that guy from *The Machinist* had a baby, and that's not a compliment."

Keira made a show of grumbling about it but broke off an edge of one of the muffins. Warm, gooey sugar filled her mouth, and she had to stop herself from shoving the whole thing in.

Zoe had leaned back in her seat and was staring at the ceiling. "You were here for that crazy storm last night, right? Blighty's a pretty wet town, but it's been a while since we've had something that heavy. My whole backyard flooded. Anyway, I woke around two in the morning. It was toward the tail end of the storm, but it was still loud enough to keep me from falling back to sleep. So I turned on a lamp and started to read my novel. I was about ready to try napping again when I heard a branch snap outside my window."

Keira's plate was empty. The second muffin waited nearby, but she stopped herself from reaching for it. "Go on."

"Well, I didn't think it was weird at first; it was a storm, and plenty of branches were breaking everywhere. But I looked out my window anyway, just in time to see this...*thing* walking past. He was so close and looking right at me. I sort of froze. Then lightning flashed and he disappeared."

"You said it looked like a dead person."

"Yeah." Zoe spread her hands. "I know it sounds crazy. And it was dark, and my window was foggy. He was only there for a second, so I guess you could argue I didn't see him clearly...but his face was bone white and all angled and narrow and horrible. Just like a skeleton."

"Huh." Keira scratched a hand through her hair as her mind whirled. It was an odd description, but the idea of a man slinking through the storm, on private property, peering into windows... *They were looking for me.*

"And before you ask, it wasn't a nightmare." Zoe rolled her eyes. "That's what everyone has been trying to tell me. But I swear, I was awake. I can even remember where I stopped reading.

It was one of the steamy parts in my book; the duchess was just about to take Lord Frederick's—"

"I believe you," Keira said quickly. "I was just thinking. The face…could it have been a mask? Or paint?"

"Yeah, that's a definite possibility. But I'm not sure if that would make it better or worse. Either way, there was something or someone in my backyard at two in the morning. I would have called the police, but they're bloody useless and never answer the phones at night." She snorted. "Plus, they've blacklisted me for too many complaints. If I'm going to get answers, it's going to have to come from somewhere else."

Keira could see where this was going. "Like from me."

"It's as I said: no one just *passes through* Blighty." Zoe propped her elbows on the table and rested her chin in her palms. "And even if they did, they wouldn't buy survival rations or look like they're expecting to be jumped any second. Don't think I haven't noticed how many times you've looked at the door."

Keira was about to insist she hadn't, but then the bell above the door jingled as it opened, and her eyes flicked toward it. It was a reflexive action.

Zoe raised her eyebrows to make her point, and Keira adjusted her hold on the mug. She wasn't sure she liked the panicked, overcautious person she seemed to be. Prudence told her to hide how she'd arrived in Blighty, but did she really have anything to lose by sharing her story? The men who had chased her were a threat, but they clearly hadn't come from the town; otherwise, Adage would have recognized them. Zoe seemed harmless, despite her intensity. And Keira hated to admit it to herself, but she really wanted another ally.

She looked back at Zoe's expectant, hopeful face and wet her lips. "Don't share any of this, okay?"

"Of course." Zoe's expression instantly switched to one of solemn duty, and Keira failed to smother a chuckle.

"Okay. This is going to sound a bit crazy."

"Oh good. That's my favorite kind of story."

Keira quickly covered the events from the previous twelve hours, starting with waking in the forest clearing and finishing with walking to town. She skipped over parts of the story that would raise too many questions—particularly the ghost outside her window, her shortage of money, and Mason's visit—but didn't hold anything else back. When she'd finished, she pushed her empty mug to one side and said, "So now I'm wondering if your skeleton man might be related. The end."

"Wow." Zoe's face was placid, except for her eyes, which were as round as marbles. "You might just be the coolest person I've ever met."

"I'm glad you think so because I feel decidedly uncool. I'm basically stuck waiting for my memories to come back or to be matched to a missing-persons report."

"Stuck in Blighty," Zoe added. "You poor soul."

She snorted. "What's so bad about it? It's a cute town."

"It's boring as hell. Seriously, you're the most interesting thing I've seen since aliens abducted my dog when I was eight."

"What?"

Zoe waved the tangent away. "You've given me plenty to think about. I'd talk more, but I really need to get back to the store. Lucas will only put up with my shenanigans for so long."

"And I need to head back to the parsonage," Keira replied. "Adage might be home by now."

"Eh, don't bank on it if he's making house calls. He'd talk a deaf man's ear off." Zoe took the napkin out from under her mug, wrapped the second muffin in it, and shoved it into Keira's jacket pocket before she could object. "If you *do* figure out who you are, would you do me a huge favor and let me know before you leave town? This world's got too many mysteries in it; I'd like to know that at least one is solved."

CHAPTER 7

KEIRA COLLECTED HER GROCERIES from the store while Zoe rescued a miserable Lucas from the checkout. The bags were heavy, but the walk to the shops had taken less than ten minutes, so Keira figured her muscles were up to the challenge.

Just like earlier, she put her head down and made herself small. She still attracted a handful of curious glances, but if Zoe had been right about Blighty's isolation, it would be impossible not to.

A teen exited the bakery ahead of her, a partially eaten frosted pastry in one hand, and turned into Keira's path. She tried to duck out of his way but was a second too late. They collided, Keira stumbled into the wall, and the teen made a choking noise as he stepped back. "What the hell!"

Keira struggled to draw breath. The impact hadn't been hard enough to do more than rob her of her balance, but it had been accompanied by something else. Something stronger. An emotion, like a punch to her stomach. Dread.

She blinked at the strange man. He seemed a year or two younger than Keira, but he had the height advantage and used it to glower down at her.

"You nearly made me drop my lunch." His lip curled up, disturbing the fuzz of a barely there mustache. "Are you going to apologize or what?"

She'd only felt it for the split second their bodies were in contact, but remnants of the sensation clung to her, like a thick, tacky oil she would never be free from. Her insides were cold, her palms sweating, every hair on her body raised.

The boy was scrawny, his overly fussy bleached hair matching a set of designer clothes. He didn't look dangerous. But her subconscious both feared and hated him.

His disgust was growing thicker, and he took a step closer. Keira reflexively moved away, putting her back to the bakery's brick wall.

"I know you heard me," he said. "Apologize."

It was a power play. He wanted to see how easily he could bend her to his will. Her subconscious had soaked in every detail about the stranger—the way he held himself; the cold, intense light in his eyes; the twist in his lips—and warned her the man blocking her path was uniquely unhinged. It would be stupid to challenge him, especially when she was trying not to draw attention to herself.

"I'm sorry we bumped into each other." It was a compromise, and the truth.

The angle of his mouth suggested he didn't appreciate her concession, but she wasn't about to let him demand more. She ducked around him and increased her pace as she walked toward the end of the main road.

He didn't follow, but she could feel the man's eyes on her back for several long moments. His stare made her skin crawl.

As she retraced the path toward the church's driveway, Keira couldn't resist glancing into the florist's. The pince-nez-wearing owner, Polly, was wrapping a bouquet for a customer. Keira found it impossible to imagine the tiny lady with permed hair and manicured nails as a vintage bank robber. Zoe had to be wrong about that, just like her subconscious was probably overreacting about the hostile man. She tried to put both thoughts out of her mind, no matter how resiliently they clung there.

It was still a chilly, damp day, but the sun had topped the trees, and Keira was sticky with sweat by the time the parsonage came into sight. She looked through the windows as she passed, but the rooms were dark and empty. As Zoe had predicted, Adage was still in town.

When Keira crossed the border into the cemetery, a slow, creeping chill slid over her. She knew it was because of the way the towering forest trees smothered the sunlight and dropped the temperature, but she couldn't repress a shudder.

Is the ghost still here, somewhere out of sight? Are there others like her? There must be at least four hundred graves here... Surely she can't be the only spirit that lingered after death.

An unnatural silence filled the space, as though stepping

through the graveyard's gate moved her into another realm—somewhere she wasn't sure she was welcome. Trees elsewhere in Blighty thrived. In this space, most had either lost their leaves early in the season or long since died.

The most direct route to the cottage involved following the ragged, age-formed pathways that wound through the stones. The only alternative would involve walking through the forest, and even there, she wouldn't be able to avoid the graves. The stones spilled beyond the bounds of the clearing. She couldn't tell how far. Either the cemetery had long since run out of room, or it had once been larger and trees had gradually encroached on the space, consuming grass and graves alike.

Keira kept her eyes focused on the little stone cottage against the forest edge and only started breathing properly again once she was inside, with the door firmly bolted behind her. Not that she expected wood and stone to do much to stop a ghost…but it felt good to be somewhere familiar. Like coming home.

Keira opened the cupboard and stacked her rice on one shelf and the potatoes on the other, then put the toothbrush and soap in the bathroom. Eating the muffin Zoe had forced into her pocket, she returned to the living room and looked around the space. The room still held a lot of the warmth from that morning's fire, even though the grate contained nothing but dull embers. She turned in a circle on the rug, searching for something that might distract her for an hour or two while she waited for Adage. The cottage didn't have any television or books that she could see, and most of the cupboards held nothing but dust.

This place needs cleaning. Keira rubbed at the back of her neck and made a face. *Not the sort of distraction I was hoping for, but it beats sitting by the window at least.*

She found gloves and old cloths under the sink, opened the windows, and set about chasing out some of the dust. On one hand, it felt silly to clean a house that would return to being abandoned within a day or two. But it was one of the few things she could do to repay Adage, and even though it in no way matched his kindness, she wanted to show him that at least she was trying.

She'd flipped the bed's mattress over and was in the process of putting on fresh sheets when a brisk knock at the door startled her. "Keira? It's Adage. I hope you got my note."

"Ah!" Keira jogged to let the pastor in. "I did, thanks. Not that it's my business to tell you what to do or anything, but is it wise to invite strangers into your home while you're out?"

Adage's face was still flushed from his walk, likely because of the bundle of cloths he carried in his arms, but he beamed at her as he stomped his boots on the mat. "Don't worry so much. I told you last night that I know everyone in town, and I'm proud to say I trust most of them a little farther than I could throw them." He extended his burden and exhaled when Keira took it from him. "Thank you, child. They're heavier than I thought they'd be."

Keira shifted the bundle a little. She could see cotton, denim, and even some lace. "What are they?"

"Clothes from our donation bin. You won't be a fashion icon, but they're clean and respectable. I guessed your size. I hope they fit."

"Seriously?" Keira lowered the clothes onto the round table. "I mean, thank you…but I don't feel right taking these."

"You're welcome to wear trash bags, if you prefer." Adage slid into the comfy lounge by the fire and exhaled a satisfied sigh as he relaxed against the pillows. "But those clothes were intended for people who couldn't easily afford their own. I don't think anyone would begrudge them going to you."

Keira swallowed as she flipped through the first few items. She hated feeling as if she was taking and taking without giving back, but it would be nice to wear something clean and soft, and the offering included a T-shirt featuring a bug-eyed cat face that she found absolutely hilarious. "Thank you."

The pastor was watching her through one eye. "You've got a little more color today. Did you have enough stew?"

"Oh, I'm good actually! I walked to town and bought some food, so I won't have to keep taking yours." Saying it gave her a little buzz of pride. "Would you like something to drink?"

"That would be lovely." The pastor's eyes had closed, and he looked as though he could happily fall asleep where he was. "Black tea with plenty of sugar, thank you. I've had the most exhausting day. Both Miss Millbury and Mrs. House wanted to see me, and I swear neither of them have any comprehension of the concept of peace, let alone know what it sounds like."

Keira had left the cups from that morning to dry on the sink, so she put a tea bag in each while the kettle boiled. "It seems like a really…interesting town. Do you know Zoe Turner? I met her when I was shopping, and she somehow got me to confess everything."

"Charming soul, that one. Accused me of being a part of a conspiracy involving highly intelligent sea mammals and Scientology." He chuckled. "She had dossiers and everything. I was quite impressed."

"Is she...uh..." The kettle finished boiling, and Keira used the interruption as an excuse to chew over how to phrase herself. "Is she an okay sort of person?"

"Oh yes, definitely. Like I said, she's a charming soul."

Keira realized, with surprise, the pastor's comment hadn't been facetious. "Really?"

"Certainly." He took the cup she passed him. "She's a little abrasive, but there are plenty of worse sins a person could indulge in. Cruelty, duplicity, small-mindedness. I've known her for her entire life, and she's never exhibited any of those. You could have a much worse friend."

That was a relief. She'd wanted to share her puzzle with Zoe, but it had still felt like a risk, and Adage's reassurance helped to erase some of her uneasiness. Keira took the wooden chair beside the pastor and blew on her cup of tea.

"There's not exactly an easy way to transition to this," Adage said, "but I made some inquiries, as promised. I'm friends with the constable, and he was able to search a database of missing persons. No one matching your description has been reported as missing within the last two weeks, but he's promised to watch it in case a new report comes through."

"Right." The news didn't come as a surprise to Keira. Everything she'd learned about herself pointed toward a nontraditional lifestyle. If anyone was missing her, they wouldn't be the sort of person to contact the police.

"I hope you'll do me the honor of staying here until we can find you a more permanent home."

Keira smiled into her tea. It was an incredibly elegant way of phrasing the offer. "You don't know how grateful I am. I'll find a way to repay you."

"Nonsense. My good deeds won't be worth half as much in the next life if I take payment for them." He winked to let her know he was joking. "Would you like me to ask around for a job and a rental place? It would probably need to be in one of the larger towns, I'm afraid. Blighty's career options aren't exactly abundant, but I'm sure I could find something suitable in Glendale or McKenzie."

Keira chewed on her lip as she turned toward the window. Deep-gray clouds had started to gather above them. The town wasn't visible from her chair, but she could still picture its lights glowing through the valley. The settlement was so picturesque that it had been easy to imagine living there. Still, beggars couldn't be choosers, and she would be grateful for any kind of stability. "That would be great."

Adage leaned back in his chair and closed his eyes. "You know, the proper, official thing to do would be to declare yourself to the police and let them look into your past. They might have better luck than I did."

Keira shook her head. "No. I'd rather not draw too much attention to myself if those men are still looking for me." *Not to mention police investigations would mean hospital investigations, questioning, searching for a match in the criminal database…*

For a second, Keira imagined how it would feel to see her mug shot appear on a police search, to hear the officers muttering as they cuffed her and dragged her toward the cells. An unpleasant taste flooded her mouth. *That's the problem with having a mystery past life—you don't know what you might be guilty of.*

"Take a day or so to rest up and get your bearings," the pastor said. "In the meantime, I'll ask around to see if I can find someone who'll take in a cheap boarder so we can get you somewhat-permanently settled."

Keira shook herself free from the unpleasant mental images. "I'd love that."

Adage drained his cup and rose. "I'd best be going then. I'm leading a study group tonight and should be preparing the material. If you want to go out again, don't leave it too late. They say we have more rain coming."

She believed it. The clouds had grown darker while they talked, and a prickling sensation over her scalp told her a storm was coming. It made her uneasy. *Why? Will rain bring the spirit back?* Her eyes flicked toward the window where she'd seen the specter. "Um, Adage?"

He stopped with his hand on the door and gave her a kindly smile. "Yes?"

She swallowed. There was no simple, offhanded way to ask what she wanted to know, so she had to trust in the pastor's unflappable congeniality to not take her question the wrong way. "Are there any ghost stories around Blighty? Around the cemetery?"

"Getting squeamish of the graves, are we?"

"No, not at all! I was just curious. I mean, a town as old as this, it's got to have some urban legends, right?"

Adage considered that for a moment. "Well, you'll always hear campfire stories, but I don't think anyone takes them seriously. If you're worried about sleeping so close to the graves, I can tell you that I've lived beside this cemetery for forty years and never seen anything of a ghostly nature."

"Okay, good." She hoped the tightness in her chest wasn't leaking into her voice. "That…puts my mind at rest."

"See you tomorrow, child."

I hope, the morbid part of her mind responded.

CHAPTER 8

KEIRA LEANED AGAINST THE window and watched Adage make his way toward his parsonage. The stones had grown long shadows over their uncut grass, and heavy clouds blanketed the sky with pending rain.

If I'm going to spend another night in this cottage, I want to know about its ghost. Who is she? What does she want?

Keira took a deep breath, crossed to the door, and let herself out. She'd forgotten how insulated the cottage was; the outside air tried to worm its way through the gaps in her clothes and chill her core. She zipped up her jacket, put her head down, and strode into the cemetery.

Although she'd been looking, she hadn't seen any sign of the ghost since the night before. She didn't know what that meant. Was the spirit dormant or sleeping? Had she moved to a different location? Or was it even possible she had relinquished her hold on the world and moved on to the next life?

Am I sure there even is *a next life?*

Keira stopped at the cottage's garden wall and rubbed her sleeve across her nose, which was growing wet. Like phantom snakes, thin tendrils of mist writhed between the stones, leaving dew wherever they touched.

Adage has never encountered a ghost, despite living here most of his life. That means the ability to see them is unique to me, not to the location. She turned in a semicircle as she examined the nearby stones. A tall cross near her gate looked at least a hundred years old, but one a few meters to her right was so clean, it could have been installed within the past year. From what she could see, very little planning had gone into the cemetery, and new graves were placed wherever there was room for them.

She began reading names as she walked among them. Occasionally, she would find husbands and wives buried together, and even family plots. The farther away from the parsonage she walked, the older the graves seemed to be. As she neared the forest, she started to find stones whose faces were so old that the words were worn off. Some had tipped over or sunk into the earth. Others were overgrown with weeds and spindly vines.

Keira paused at the edge of the forest. She raised her eyes, and chills slipped through her in waves as she stared into the tangle of trees and grave markers. The stones were all old, and many had crumbled, but they seemed to go on forever. In some cases, trees had collapsed over the slabs, crushing them, or the markers had fallen over and depressed into the forest floor to become morbid stepping stones.

She pushed forward, moving carefully to avoid stepping on any overgrown graves, one arm raised to push spiky, dead branches away from her face. She wanted to see how deep into the woods the graves went and whether the cemetery truly had an end. Light faded as the trees closed in behind her, and yet the stone markers still surrounded her, listing, rotting, half-consumed by the earth, going on for as far as her eyes could make out.

A whispered noise echoed from ahead. It sent a spike of fear through Keira. A coppery taste flooded her mouth and made her stomach clench.

There's something evil here. Something evil…something evil… something evil…

The thought echoed again and again, becoming a mantra she couldn't silence. The ground ahead of her was tainted with more than just bones. A dark figure shifted between distant trees.

Something evil…something evil…something evil…

She staggered backward, her heart a staccato pulse in her ears, her breathing ragged. She barely noticed as branches snagged at her clothes and kept moving even when she'd passed out of the forest's border. The backs of her legs hit a solid object; she fell over it, tumbling to the spongy earth as she raised her hands to guard her face.

Her mind fell silent. The fear abated, moving out of her in a steady ebb, until all that remained were the shaking hands and racing pulse. Something sharp and cold pinged off her forehead, then another hit her hand. It had started raining.

Slowly, as though sudden movements could undo the calm,

Keira lifted her torso off the ground. She'd tripped over a low, square tombstone. Horror impacted her as she realized she was on top of a grave, and she scrambled back, desperate to get onto clean ground.

Thunder rumbled in the distance. She came to rest in a space between two graves and wrapped her arms around her chest. The forest waited ahead of her, dark and dripping with malaise.

What was that? Something moved between the trees, and it didn't seem human…

The rain was coming down in cold, hard spits, coating her hair and trickling down the back of her neck. Keira shuddered and blew out a breath. It plumed in front of her. The temperature was plummeting with unnatural speed.

An eerie sensation crawled over Keira's skin. She twisted to look behind herself, but she was alone.

No, her instincts whispered. *You're not.*

"Hello?" More condensation came out with the word. The fog was thickening, transforming from tendrils into an ocean, and the continued drop in temperature made her shiver uncontrollably. She squinted, trying to pick shapes out of the mist.

Then she blinked, and something inside of her head clicked. It was like a Magic Eye poster. The picture appeared as a jumble of nothing until she looked at it in exactly the right way, then the hidden image became clear.

The woman, so transparent that her floating hair and sundress were almost invisible, walked through the markers a row ahead of Keira. Her delicate, bloodied face twisted as she wrung her hands.

Keira didn't dare speak, didn't dare move, but stayed huddled on the ground, half-obscured by the fog. The idea to search for the ghost had seemed logical while she was inside the cottage, but crouched among the gravestones as the light failed and a storm brewed overhead, the notion felt positively insane.

The woman didn't seem to notice Keira. She strode along a row of graves, turned, and paced back the way she came from. Her lips moved, but the words were inaudible. The sticky bone fragments of her crushed skull glistened in the dim light.

Keira had to strain to keep the transient figure in her vision. It was as though she had a muscle just behind her eyes that made the ghost visible. As soon as she relaxed it, the woman disappeared into the mist.

She blinked, mentally collected herself, and tried again, focusing on using the muscle she hadn't even known existed. It took a moment, but then the woman emerged back into her vision, standing directly ahead of Keira and gazing toward town.

They were close. Keira could feel a chill rolling off the spirit and reflexively leaned away from it. The movement drew the woman's notice, and her head snapped toward Keira. The long, blood-streaked hair swirled like a cloud behind her.

They watched each other, both silent, both waiting. Keira felt as though she was supposed to say something, but words died on her tongue. Her body shook from the cold as stress and fear clouded her head, but she knew she couldn't leave. Not yet.

Then the dead woman turned and began walking along the row of graves, unconcerned that she was treading over the burials. She stopped and looked over her shoulder, her expression beseeching. A request to follow.

On unsteady legs, Keira rose. The drizzle had soaked into her clothes and made her feel heavy, but when she took a step toward the ghost, the woman turned and continued. As she walked through the fog, her body took on a luminescent sheen, and her form's solidity waxed and waned according to the mist's density.

Although the ghost walked across the graves, Keira took care not to step on them. She couldn't even tell herself why, but it seemed disrespectful to walk over the coffins, like desecrating sacred ground. She had to weave around the graves and even climb over two hedges to keep up with the spirit.

They were moving toward the forest's edge. Keira's anxiety increased as they drew nearer to it. *Please, not into the woods…*

The woman stopped and turned. She waited for Keira to catch up, then gave a graceful nod toward the shape beside her.

She was standing on a grave. The stone was small and modest, a traditional curved-top slab without adornments. Keira had to move closer to the spirit than she was comfortable with in order to read the words carved on it.

Emma Carthage 1955–1981

"Is this yours?" Keira looked up, but the woman was gone. Keira took a step back as she looked around herself. "Emma?"

No answer came from the garden of gravestones.

"I'm going to try to help." Keira's voice came out faint, so she licked her dry lips and tried again. "I have your name now. I'll find out who you were in life and how you died, and…I can't promise… I don't know how much I can do…but whatever you need, I'll try to get it for you."

Still no response. Keira felt for the muscle behind her eyes and strained it, pushing as hard as she could as she looked over the graveyard. There was a flicker of motion somewhere to her right. No—there was a shape to her left, fading as soon as she tried to look at it.

The rapidly advancing twilight made it difficult to see. She tried harder. A throbbing headache began at the back of her skull and flared over her scalp. She pushed through it, fighting to get both her internal and external eyes to work in tandem and show her the woman. It felt like straining against an invisible wall. The barrier cracked, then broke, and Keira was suddenly able to look through.

She inhaled and stumbled backward. Her shoulders hit a tree, and she pressed herself against it, her heart thundering, her head burning from the strain. For only a second, she'd seen them: Blighty Cemetery's ghosts, deformed, discontent, and scattered among the graves, watching her. There had been dozens of them.

"Oh," Keira whispered. Her lungs were burning, and she had to force herself to draw breath. The specters had faded as soon as she'd relaxed the second sight, but she knew they were still there, surrounding her, waiting to reach their long fingers through the mist and snag her limbs as she passed them.

Keira put her head down and ran. Despite the numbing cold and fear, her legs carried her in long lopes across the graveyard. She darted around the headstones and over long-dead flower beds, eyes squinted against the drizzling rain. She didn't allow herself to think about what she was passing through, didn't even try to look for it, as she raced for her home.

She hit the cottage's door with a bang and fumbled to turn the handle. A draft of warm air welcomed her as she slipped inside. She closed and locked the door, then almost laughed at herself. *Yes, because a latch will definitely keep the ghosts out.*

Keira put a hand to her forehead and sucked in long, shaky breaths. Exhaustion and stress drained her. The headache, caused by opening her eyes to the spirits, continued to throb at the back of her skull.

Am I alone in here? Do I want to know if I'm not?

She ran a hand through her wet hair and groaned. She wouldn't be able to sleep in the cottage if it contained ghosts. The headache flared when she flexed the muscle behind her eyes, but she forced it to work, pushing it as hard as she could.

Her room was empty.

It was agonizing to hold the sight, but she didn't relax it immediately. Instead, she turned to the window and looked through. The cemetery's spirits were barely visible. A few had almost-defined forms, but most were shimmers of light among the mist. They filled the graveyard, but none came past the cottage garden's wall.

Perhaps the dead have a sense of respect for the living too. Keira exhaled as she relaxed her vision, and the shapes disappeared. She slumped against the wall, letting her eyes close. She felt wrung out and sore, as if she could sleep for a lifetime.

The rain wasn't as intense as it had been the night before but fell in a slow, steady drizzle. She hoped it would be clear the next day. She wasn't sure she wanted to spend much more time trapped in the cottage and surrounded by the graveyard.

As the headache subsided, Keira stumbled toward the fire. The coals were close to dead but still retained some of their heat. She managed to revive the blaze, in spite of her questionable method of just shoving in whatever wood was close to hand.

Keira put the kettle on as she passed it, then began pulling off her soaked outfit. She was grateful she'd accepted Adage's donation of clothes. A thick sweater was included, and she pulled it on, along with a pair of black jeans that were a few sizes too large.

As she draped the wet clothes over the chair to dry, a faint noise reached her through the rain's patter. Keira fell still and held her breath as she listened. The sound repeated, almost inaudible but horribly persistent. It sounded like fingernails being dragged across wood.

Keira turned toward the door. Her pulse kicked up again as the sound came once more. Slowly, rolling her feet to muffle her footsteps, she crept toward the window and craned her neck to look through.

Night had fallen, and the black clouds blotted out every hint of moonlight. She didn't think anyone was outside the door, but it was hard to be sure when the window's light only touched part of her stoop.

Is it a ghost? Keira moved away from the window, sickened by the idea that whoever or whatever was outside could watch her without being observed in turn. *I didn't think they could touch physical objects.*

The scratching noise came louder. Whatever it was, it wanted to come in.

CHAPTER 9

KEIRA STARED AT THE door handle. Her instincts told her not to open it. Whatever was outside might not be human, and even if it was, that didn't mean it was friendly.

But the only alternative was to ignore it, and she didn't think that would fly. It knew the building was occupied; the lights in the windows and smoke from the chimney were more than enough evidence. And if it truly wanted to come inside, invited or not…

The scratching came again, more insistent. Then it was followed by a new sound: a tiny, peeping cry. It was at odds with the scratching noise, but all at once familiar. The tension drained out of Keira. She exhaled a shaky laugh as she unlocked and opened the door.

For a second, she saw nothing outside except inky black. Then two large yellow eyes blinked into view, followed by twitching ears and the long, lithe body of a scrawny black cat. It gave Keira the briefest glance possible, then trotted past her, aimed toward the fire like a heat-seeking missile.

Keira grinned and shook her head as she closed the door against the rain and cold. "You frightened me, little guy. What are you doing outside in weather like this?"

The ears twitched at her voice, but the cat didn't turn around. It stopped in front of the fire, watching the flickering flames, then lay down in the most absurd way Keira had ever seen. The head went down first, thumping into the carpet, and the shoulders and torso followed, then finally the hind legs. The cat flopped out to its full length, exposing its belly to the heat, and released an audible exhale.

Keira couldn't stop smiling at the sight. She went to the bathroom and found a towel, then gently approached the cat.

"Hey, little guy," she said, keeping her voice light as she moved nearer. "You're kinda wet. Will you let me dry you?"

He paid her no attention but stretched into the touch when Keira brushed the towel along his back. She knelt next to him and tried to dry the drenched black fur as well as she could. *He must be someone's pet to be this tame. But we're pretty far from town. How'd he get out here?*

The cat rolled onto his back and stretched his paws into the air. Keira felt a low, rapid rumble under her hands as he started to purr.

"You're very cute," she murmured, scratching under his chin. He responded by leaning his head back and sticking the tip of his tongue out between his teeth. "In a weird sort of way."

She didn't think he was fully grown. The cat's body was long and bony, and he seemed to be in that intermediate stage where he wasn't quite an adult cat but was past being a kitten. She hoped he would stay for the rest of the night. It would be nice to have some company, especially considering what was waiting outside.

The memory of the spirits hovering among the graves flashed through her mind, and Keira squeezed her lips together. She couldn't do a thing about it, so she tried not to dwell on them and instead turned her mind toward the most persistent presence.

I have a name now: Emma Carthage. This is a small town; even though Emma died decades ago, someone should still remember her.

Her hand had fallen still, and the cat used its head to butt at the towel in a demand for more attention. She obliged.

I wonder why I could see her but not the other ghosts. Is she stronger? Or did she just really, really want to be seen? She snorted. *Old Keira probably knew the hows and whys. Old Keira probably knew lots of things, like the most efficient way to shank someone.*

"What am I going to do, cat?"

The black creature still had its tongue poking out. The pink contrasted fantastically with his black fur, and his pupils were gradually drifting in different directions as he relaxed. He looked truly demented. Keira bopped his nose, then rose to take the towel back to the laundry. It had developed a distinctive wet-cat smell, so she put it in the washer.

"What am I going to do?" she repeated to her reflection. Big, doleful eyes blinked back, and she narrowed them in an attempt to look fierce. The effect bordered on comedic, so she huffed a sigh and returned to the living room.

She'd told the ghost she would try to help, but that was easier said than done. The spirit hadn't been able to communicate what kept it trapped on earth, but Keira could make an educated guess. Emma had been murdered. She wanted her killer brought to justice.

Hunger gnawed at her, so Keira set up a pot with rice to boil, then checked on her guest. The cat had contorted into an awkward, yoga-esque pose but looked happy enough. Keira sat next to him and watched his whiskers twitch as he dreamed.

She died more than forty years ago. If the police didn't catch the killer back then, what chance do I have of piecing together clues now? Everything will either be eroded by time or held at a police station. And there's the very real chance that the killer might already be dead. Forty years is a long time.

"Stop complaining, Keira," she told herself, and she stretched her bare feet toward the flames. "You've got something the police never had: the key witness."

Although Emma couldn't speak, she could move, point, nod, and shake her head. That would be plenty to help Keira narrow down the suspects. Once she identified them, at least.

First order of business: find out how much of Emma's story was public knowledge. Adage would probably know, plus Mason had said he would visit the following morning, and, in a pinch, Zoe could probably throw around some wild theories.

The hardest part would be coming up with a convincing

excuse for asking. "Hey, so a ghost wants me to figure out who killed her" probably wouldn't get her investigation far.

A hissing noise sent her scrambling for the stove. The pot had boiled over while she was lost in thought, and Keira quickly dumped the steaming rice into a bowl. She didn't notice until she sat back in front of the fire that it hadn't fully cooked, and by then she was feeling too sleepy and lazy to put it back on to boil. The rice was crunchy but edible, so she finished the bowl while massaging the cat with her feet. He'd dried quickly in the fire's heat and was pleasantly warm. She hoped his owner wasn't missing him. He seemed comfortable in the cottage and had claimed the spot in front of the fire as though he slept there every night.

It must be nice to feel like you belong somewhere. That you're not inconveniencing other people or taking things you don't deserve.

She snorted a laugh. *You're getting awfully maudlin there, Keira. Time for some rest.*

CHAPTER 10

SLEEP DIDN'T WANT TO release Keira from its grip. Something was poking at her back, but she just batted it away and grumbled as she tried to fall back under. A cold, scratchy object touched her cheek. Groaning, Keira recoiled, then cracked her eyes open to see what was assaulting her.

Pale morning sunlight came through the cottage's windows and painted the room in washed-out tones. She'd fallen asleep in the bed—something her back thanked her for—and the scrawny, big-eared cat perched on the mattress's edge as it blinked its huge, liquid-amber eyes at her.

"Please, not yet," she mumbled as the cold nose came in to nuzzle at her cheek again. "I'm tired."

He responded by climbing onto her back and kneading at the space between her shoulder blades. Keira squeaked as the claws made it through her sweater and poked at her skin and carefully rolled him off. "Okay, okay, you win. Let's go out."

She rubbed sleep out of her eyes as she shuffled to the door. The cat followed her at a quick trot, tail held up like a flag, head swiveling as he watched her. Keira braced herself against the cold and opened the door. "There you go, buddy. Safe journey."

He ignored the door and continued to stare at her. Keira shivered as cold air rushed through the opening. "Isn't this what you wanted?"

His mouth opened, and he exhaled the tiniest, squeakiest mewl imaginable. Keira grimaced and closed the door. Her brain was starting to wake up, and its deductions weren't good news. The cat didn't want to leave; he was hungry.

All I have is rice and potatoes, and neither of those is remotely appropriate for cats.

She ran a hand over her face. The simplest solution would be to return the cat to its owner, but she had no idea who that was. She couldn't go door-to-door searching, especially not at such an early hour, and double especially not while carrying the feline. It would be cruel to boot him out of the cottage and even crueler not to give him anything to eat. But she had no money left to buy him food.

There was only one option left, and it wasn't remotely appealing. She would have to beg.

"Crap." Keira collected her boots from the fireplace and pulled them on. They were still damp. It was another big tick in the "how to have a bad morning" checklist, and Keira scrunched up her face as she pulled a spare hoodie over her sweater and stepped into the freezing morning.

The rain had receded but left heavy, low clouds and thick, white mist in its place. Keira fixed her attention on the ground as she jogged through the cemetery. She found it easier to keep moving if her eyes weren't trying to pick out shapes amid the swirling fog.

She kept her pace brisk, and her core had warmed by the time she reached the main stretch of road leading into town, even if her nose was dripping and her fingers were numb. She slowed to a walk and looked into the first store she passed, the florist. Bouquets covered every visible surface in the tiny shop, but the lights were off and the possibly-a-bank-robber pince-nez-wearing owner was nowhere to be seen.

I didn't realize it was so early. What time do the Blighty stores open?

She turned toward the central fountain. The streets were empty, and she hoped she wouldn't look too out of place if she sat on the fountain's edge while she waited for the general store to open its doors.

To her surprise, a voice called her name just as she was crossing the street. Zoe, bundled in gloves, a beanie, and a long coat, waved to her from near the general store.

"Good morning!" Zoe's round face was pink from the cold, but her grin was huge. "You're up early."

"I was about to say the same to you."

"Eh, I like to get here before the crowds. I make a coffee and read the newspapers." She winked as she unlocked the store's door. "I'm working on a collage demonstrating how the U.S. government has been systematically infecting tofu in order to experiment on the vegan population, and you never know when you might find a piece of evidence in a seemingly innocent news article."

Keira was tempted to laugh but didn't want to offend her companion. "Wow. That sounds…intense."

"Oh, it is. There're hints that they were planning to use mass-spread hallucinogenics to fake the moon landing, but it ended up being cheaper to send someone to the moon for real. C'mon in. Were you after more rice or something?"

Keira flexed her shoulders as she entered the store. The lights came on in sporadic bursts, flickering as though reluctant to be woken. The cluttered space looked strange when it was void of other shoppers, as though it belonged in a dystopian world. "I found a little black cat last night. Well, technically, he found me. Could you keep an ear out for anyone who might have lost him?"

"Can do." Zoe shed her jacket and dropped it behind the counter. She leaned against the counter as she flexed her shoulders. "Is it super fat? That might be the Torries'. Or if it had a white nose and paws, that'd be the Childs'."

"Sorry, it's completely black and small. Kind of scrawny."

Zoe shrugged. "Doesn't ring any bells, but I'll ask around. Did you want some coffee or anything?"

Keira cleared her throat. She'd had the entire walk to decide how she should phrase herself, but the words were still difficult to say. "He needs something to eat. But I can't afford to buy anything right now. Is it possible… I mean, would you consider giving me some food for him? Even meat scraps would be okay."

Zoe's expression was impossible to read. She tilted her head to one side and pursed her lips. After a second, she said, "How about a trade?"

Keira found it hard to meet the other woman's eyes. "I…don't have much to give. I could clean the store. Or get you the money later—"

"Nah, I was thinking more along the lines of coffee."

"Huh?"

Zoe shrugged artlessly. "Let me buy you a coffee again. I spent half of last night thinking up theories about how you ended up in Blighty, and I'm literally dying to run some of them past you."

The offer seemed too good. Keira raised a skeptical eyebrow. "That's all?"

"Look, you don't even need to do it if you really don't want to. I'll still give you the cat food. I'm not a monster. Jeez."

Before Keira could object, Zoe grabbed her sleeve and dragged her farther into the store. She snagged a basket on the way past and shoved it into Keira's other hand. "We'll get him some dry and some wet, so he can choose his favorite. And treats. Cats love treats."

The anxiety bled out of Keira as she watched her basket being filled. "Hey, we don't need all this. Just enough food to last a day or two until I can find his owner."

Zoe plucked a pack of cat toys off the shelf and threw them on top of the food. "Better to be prepared."

Keira shook her head incredulously. "Prepared for what? The zombie apocalypse?"

"Yeah, either that or the AI-sentience Armageddon. It's really a toss-up for which will happen first."

At that, Keira had no hope of holding in her laughter, but Zoe didn't seem to care. She maintained her grip on Keira's sleeve and pulled her back to the register. "I'll get these bagged up for you. So is that a yes for coffee? The café doesn't open for like half an hour, but I bet I can bust down the back door and disable the alarm—"

"No! That's okay!" Keira, concerned by the turn the conversation had taken, jogged to keep up with the sales assistant. "I can meet you there later."

Zoe's shoulders slumped. "Ugh, but I won't be free again until my lunch break, and that's literally *hours* away."

"Work on your doomsday plans until then," Keira suggested. "I want to get this food back to the cat. Besides, I'm expecting a visitor, and I don't know how early he'll come."

"A visitor?" Zoe's miserable expression morphed into keen interest. "And it's a *he*? Who? Is it your handler? If you squint your eyes, does he start to look like a reptile?"

"Nothing like that. He's just one of Adage's acquaintances."

"Ahh." Zoe nodded, as though this answered everything. A mischievous smile pulled at her bright-red lips. "Good old Adage. Must be playing matchmaker again. Is the guy cute at least?"

Keira hated the direction the conversation was turning, but Zoe had leaned one arm against the opposite aisle, blocking Keira's access to the door. "Don't make such a big deal out of it. He's just seeing if he can help with the lost memories. Mason's studying to be a doctor."

Zoe's smile vanished. "Mason Corr? You're kidding." She frowned but didn't move out of Keira's way. For the first time, Keira thought she'd genuinely caught Zoe off-guard.

"Is there something wrong?"

"Eh." Zoe rolled her shoulders, squinting toward the ceiling. "I guess it makes sense that Adage would call him. Adage hates the doctor—like, really, really hates him—and he's always had a soft spot for Mason. But, Keira, do me a favor, okay?"

"Yeah?"

"You might want to watch your back around him."

Keira glanced toward the window. The street was starting to fill with early morning traffic. Some of the couples talked and laughed as they went to open their stores, but the pleasant atmosphere didn't reach inside the general store. "Why? He seemed nice yesterday."

"Yeah, he always does. He's the town's darling; he could probably charm the saltiest old maid if he tried."

"But…?"

Zoe glanced about the store, as though there might be curious ears listening in. "Do you know much about him?"

"Almost nothing."

"Well, he spent the last four years working toward becoming a doctor. First an undergraduate degree, then med school. Consistently at the top of his class. He was Blighty's brightest shooting star, destined to make a name for himself in a fancy city somewhere. Then, near the end of the year, he dropped out."

Keira shifted the shopping bags uneasily. "Why?"

"That's the million-dollar question." Zoe raised her hands in a shrug, then dropped them again. "People asked, but he either changes the subject or gives vague excuses like 'taking a break' and 'considering my options.' I heard he even got letters from his professors asking him to come back, to complete his degree—but he's been home for eight weeks now, with no signs of leaving."

"Huh." Keira chewed that over. "That *is* weird. Maybe he got burned-out?"

"And couldn't have survived a couple more months after four *years*?" Zoe made a noise that was somewhere between derision and annoyance. "Look, I'm not telling you to shun him or anything, but…just be cautious. He's hiding something. And in my calculated opinion, there's an extremely high chance that he's a serial killer who had to flee the campus in fear of being caught."

That was a segue and a half. Keira spluttered a laugh, hoisted her bags, and ducked around Zoe to reach the door. "I don't know about that. But thanks for looking out for me."

Zoe huffed a sigh, then waved Keira out of the door. "Whatever. My lunch break is at one. Meet me at the café. And remember: I will be extremely displeased if you get yourself murdered by any would-be doctor before then."

"Same to you," Keira called over her shoulder as she turned toward the cemetery.

CHAPTER 11

BLIGHTY WAS WAKING UP. Shop doors were opening and bleary-eyed townspeople were shuffling about their early-morning errands, though the roads were still near empty. Keira noted there were very few cars. She supposed most people lived close enough to the town center to walk there.

The Two Bees florist, Polly Kennard, was setting out buckets of flowers at the front of her store. Keira lowered her head and set her gaze on the ground, intending to pass the shop quickly, but she had to pull up short as a bunch of daisies was thrust across her path.

"This is the *third* time I've seen you," Polly said, leaning into Keira's field of vision. The sunlight sparkled off the florist's glasses and bleached-white teeth and made her permed hair look like cotton candy plopped on top of her head. "Are you staying in town, dear?"

"Just passing through!" The excuse was carrying less and less weight the longer Keira stayed in Blighty, but she hadn't prepared any alternatives.

"Visiting family, perhaps? How lovely." Polly's wide smile seemed both genuine and grandmotherly, and Keira tried her hardest not to visualize the woman fleeing from a bank heist. "Who are you staying with?"

"Um, with Mr. Adage."

Polly nodded as though that wasn't at all surprising. "He's a good fellow, the pastor. Well, I won't keep you. I just wanted to say hello and welcome you to our town. Why don't you take these? They match your pretty eyes."

To Keira's shock, the bunch of flowers were dropped into her shopping bag before she could reply. "Uh, thank y—"

"Of course, dear. And if you get lonely while you're here, I'd be glad to introduce you to Harry, my son." Her sharp eyes scanned Keira in a flash. "He's about your age, and he's really quite a charming gentleman."

Aha. She has a motive. Keira kept her tone light. "That's really kind of you."

Polly's eyes scrunched up as she smiled. "Anytime, dear, just pop in anytime."

Keira waited until she was out of earshot, then exhaled. *So that was Zoe's fearsome ex-outlaw. She seems sweet. Even if she's trying to set me up with her son.* Keira peeked at the flowers in her shopping bag. They were fresh and bright, but she couldn't imagine how Polly thought they matched her eyes. The daisies were pure white, save for their dark centers. *Maybe she meant they match my pupils?* Keira had to squeeze her lips together to contain the laughter.

She wasn't sure she wanted the flowers in the cottage. It felt too permanent, like she was transforming the temporary shelter into a home. She had another idea for them, though, and quickened her pace as she turned into the driveway that led to the church.

Despite the chilly wind and subdued bird chatter ringing from the trees, Keira spent most of the walk buried in thought. *Be careful around Mason.* The warning hung in her mind, but she found it hard to feel any conviction in it—partly because Zoe's theories tended toward the bizarre, if not downright ridiculous, but mostly because Mason's easy, open smile had felt too warm to be fake.

There's no reason to think he has anything to hide. Surely it's not that unusual to drop out of school, even late in the year? He was probably burned-out or realized it was the wrong career for him. And as for Zoe's theory...

Keira huffed and readjusted her grip on the bags. They were heavy; Zoe must have collected more cat food than Keira had thought. That would be okay. She'd just return the surplus once she found the cat's owner.

As she entered the graveyard, she caught sight of a figure leaned against the stone wall. She recognized the long legs and dark-chocolate hair from a distance, and quickened into a jog. Mason had his hands in his pockets and had left his medical kit beside his crossed ankles. He grinned and pushed away from the wall as she neared him.

"I'm sorry for making you wait!"

"Not at all. I was admiring the view." He motioned toward the gravestones. "It's quite…morbid."

She laughed, opened the cottage door, then stepped back so Mason could follow her in.

He shed his coat and hung it over the chair's back before turning his smile onto her. "How's your arm?"

"I kind of forgot it was a thing, actually." Keira flexed her shoulder and felt a twinge of pain but nothing distracting. "You can have the painkillers back."

"Huh. You're a tough cookie, aren't you?" He set the kit on the wooden chair's seat. "Mind if I have a look at it?"

"Sure, but give me a second first. I've been shopping for a cat that came in last night, and he's probably hungry."

As if on cue, a muted mewl came from the room's corner. Keira peered into the shadows above the wardrobe and smiled as two liquid-amber eyes blinked back, watching the humans with great interest.

Mason chuckled as he stretched to retrieve the cat. "It's cute. Looks young too."

"That's what I thought." Keira put her shopping on the kitchen counter and fetched a plate from the cupboard. "You don't know who he belongs to, do you?"

"I'm afraid not. But I'll keep an ear out for news of a missing cat."

"Thanks." Keira was sorely tempted to laugh as Mason cradled the cat like a baby, with one hand scratching behind its ears. The cat clawed at his shirt buttons as its tail twitched eagerly.

"My parents owned a cat when I was growing up," he said. "He passed away while I was in med school, and honestly, he's one of the things I miss most since coming back."

"You're a cat person, huh?"

"Oh, definitely. So many people think they're aloof, but Ruffles could have beaten a lot of dogs in the affection department. What about you? Cats or dogs?"

"Uh…" Keira took a moment to sift through the deepest parts of her mind she could reach. "I *think* I'm a cat person. I'm going to miss this guy when he goes at least. It was nice having him around."

"Looks like she's a lady actually." The black creature was gnawing on Mason's thumb, but he didn't seem to mind. "And a very friendly one at that."

"A girl, huh? I should've checked. She certainly seems to like you." Keira was having too much fun watching Mason play with the cat and turned back to the shopping before it became obvious that she was staring. She picked out the closest can and frowned at the label. It advertised pickled beetroots.

"Oh, you've got to be kidding me…" As Keira dug through the shopping, she found the reason for why the bags felt so heavy. At some point between picking up the basket and handing Keira the filled bags, Zoe had managed to sneak half a dozen cans of vegetables and fish into the shopping.

"Everything okay, Keira?"

"Oh, yeah, it's fine. Just coming to terms with the fact that I befriended a ninja." Keira let her words drop into grumbles as she pulled the cans out. *I have my own food. All I needed was something for the cat.*

Mason gracefully ignored her mutters. He came up beside her, still cradling the feline in one arm, to fill a bowl with water. Keira picked out one of the cat food cans and pulled open the lid. The cat turned from a malleable lump of squishy fur in Mason's arms into a writhing ball of energy. It squirmed out of his grip and dropped to the ground with a loud thump before bouncing to its feet.

"Yikes," she said, shaking the food onto the plate as the cat weaved around her legs. "You must be hungry. Poor thing."

She put the plate on the ground, and the cat buried its face in it. The sight sent a gnawing sense of guilt digging into her stomach. *How long has she been without food?*

She looked up and realized Mason had been watching her. His expression had lost its warmth and seemed to hold something deeply sad and dissatisfied. It was an unpleasant contrast to his usual cheerfulness, and she clutched around for something to distract him with. "I've been wasting your time. You didn't come here to feed my cat."

He smiled at that, and some of the warmth returned. "Ha, don't worry about it. This is hardly a waste. But let's have a look at that war wound."

They took the same seats as they had the day before. Keira pulled off the sweaters, and Mason burst out laughing.

"What?" She blinked, surprised, as Mason's whole body shook with his chuckles.

"Oh, you're definitely a cat person. How can you not be with a shirt like that?"

She looked down at her chest. The bug-eyed cat design stared back at her, and she sent Mason a wicked grin. "Don't laugh. It's the best T-shirt I've ever seen. I fully intend to wear it around town and make everyone jealous and start a fashion revolution."

Laughing too hard to focus on her shoulder, he had to lean his forehead against the chair's back. The mirth was infectious, and Keira couldn't resist watching him as his cheeks turned pink and his shoulders shook. But as his chuckles subsided and he straightened to examine the stitched cut, she couldn't wipe away the memory of how dark his eyes had looked just moments before. As though he truly was hiding something.

"This is looking good," Mason said. His hands were warm against her skin.

Keira didn't know where to look—at the fingers gently prodding around the stitches, at Mason's face, or at the cold fire grate. She settled on the final option but couldn't stop glancing at the man leaning close. "There's no sign of infection, so I'm really happy about that. Keep it clean, rest up, et cetera. We can take the stitches out in a few days."

He poured antiseptic onto a cotton ball and dabbed around the area before reapplying the bandages. "How are you finding Blighty? Not too dull, I hope?"

"I kind of have the opposite problem." *Gunmen, conspiracy*

theorists, ghosts—there's not much room for boredom here. Keira licked her lips. She'd been looking for an opening to ask about the cemetery's resident spirit. Mason's question didn't offer a perfect transition, but it was close enough for her to try. "Actually, I was browsing the graveyard yesterday…"

His eyes brightened with barely contained amusement. "Browsing? Like a library?"

She snorted. "Okay, that came out wrong. I was *exploring* the graveyard. Better?"

"Much."

"I found one name that sounded familiar: Emma Carthage. I'm sure I've heard it before. You don't know who she was, do you?" She instantly felt guilty about the lie as Mason's expression lit up.

"Really? Recalling names is a very good sign. Can you try to feel around it and pick up on any emotions or memories attached to it?"

"Uh—" She hoped she wasn't turning red from the shame. "I mean, it's not like a memory or anything—it just seemed a bit familiar. I was wondering if I might have heard it somewhere. Maybe in town…"

His head tilted to one side as she backpedaled. She was learning to associate the gesture with curiosity and knew he didn't fully believe her excuses. To her surprise, though, all he said was, "Emma Carthage is a bit of a local legend. It was before my time, but I can tell you what I know if you like? It's somewhat of a long story."

"I've got all the time in the world."

CHAPTER 12

MASON CLOSED THE LID on his kit and set it beside his feet. He leaned back in the chair and tapped on his lip, apparently absorbed in thought. "I've heard the story a few times, but mostly when I was a child, so the details are muddy."

"Take your time." Keira pulled her sweater back on over the bug-eyed cat shirt and settled in for the tale.

"I think I need to give you some context first. Blighty was founded by a gentleman called Mortimer Crispin. He built a wool mill and bought the farmland surrounding it, then tempted people to settle in the area with lucrative job offers. It turned out to be a profitable idea, and his already considerable wealth increased substantially before his death.

"The company was eventually closed, and the mill abandoned. Because Blighty had relied heavily on the Crispins' business, most people expected it to become a ghost town within a few years.

But for one reason or another, a large section of the population decided to stay. Some commute to the cities, others set up their own small or home businesses, and Blighty is… Well, *thriving* is a bit of a strong word, but *surviving* sounds too dire. It's existing, I guess, pretty much the same as it has for several generations."

Keira kicked off her boots and pulled her feet up underneath herself as she leaned forward. "Do the Crispins still live here?"

"Only one: Dane Crispin. He still lives in Mortimer's old house near the abandoned mill. He doesn't work, and there are rumors that the Crispin fortune has run low. Dane's sold several parcels of the family's land over the last decade."

Licking its lips, the black cat appeared beside Mason's chair. It arched its back, then leaped into his lap. Mason waited for the cat to settle before continuing. "In the seventies and early eighties, the family consisted of a gentleman named George and his three adult children. I never met him, but people have described George as arrogant. He seemed to truly believe his family was superior to those in the town simply because they had money. Out of his three children, he favored the eldest, Frank.

"From all accounts, Frank was a hardworking and kind person. If people ever talked about his faults, it was that he was too easily swayed by his father's iron will. George expected his son to marry into one of the larger cities' tycoon banking families, but his plans were scuttled when Frank fell in love with one of the local girls."

It was easy to see where this story was heading. "Emma Carthage."

"Bingo. She was beautiful, but George was livid when he found out. The Carthages were a poor family, descended from a worker in Mortimer's mill. To George, tying the families together would be a humiliating debasement, and he did everything possible to prevent it, including threatening to disown his son and promising to ruin the Carthage family.

"When Frank and Emma realized George would never relent, they planned a secret wedding. George discovered the plans and locked his son in the house on the day they were supposed to elope. He then went to see the Carthage family with an offer: he would give them a small fortune if they removed their daughter from the town."

"Oh," Keira muttered. "They didn't accept, did they?"

Mason gave her a tight-lipped smile. "They did. The family was gone the next morning."

"Wow."

"No one knows where they went. Frank maintained that he intended to marry Emma as soon as he found her, but over the following six months, his father wheedled and threatened and cajoled so severely that Frank began to talk of his love less and less."

"Emma came back, though, didn't she? Her grave's just outside."

"You're right. While her side of the story isn't so well-known, it seems she never stopped loving Frank. When he didn't come to find her, she left her family and went looking for *him*. It's suspected that she traveled on foot through the back roads because the first sighting of her was by the Crispins' groundskeeper, who saw her emerge from the woods surrounding the property and walk toward the mansion."

Keira had a sickening idea of what came next. "She didn't find Frank, though."

"No. George discovered her in the garden behind the house. They argued. He was incensed. She refused to leave without seeing Frank. So George picked up one of the rocks lining the path—"

"And beat her head in," Keira murmured, absorbed in thought.

Mason raised an eyebrow. "That's right... Good guess. The groundskeeper fetched the police. They arrived in time to find George digging a grave-sized hole in the garden. He didn't try to deny the murder. The only thing he said as they took him away was 'I wish I'd done it sooner.'"

Keira shuddered. "What a pleasant soul. What happened to him?"

"Life imprisonment, no parole. He passed away about five years ago from heart failure."

"Will I sound like a horrible person if I say good riddance?"

Mason laughed. "You'll only be echoing the sentiments of most of the town. That's not quite the end of the story, though."

"Oh no. I'd almost forgotten about Frank."

"Out of everyone, I think he may have suffered the most. He was in the house when his father murdered his intended but didn't hear about what had happened until the police called everyone out for questioning. He stayed just long enough to see that Emma was buried in this very graveyard, then walked to the abandoned mill behind the house, found a length of rope, tied one end around the rafters, and fashioned the other into a noose."

"Ah."

"Yeah. It took a few days for his body to be found. Although he'd left a note asking to be buried beside Emma, his siblings chose to put him in the family plot. They also supported their father through his unsuccessful legal battle.

"There's not much to the story after that. The Crispins, who had been one of the most respected families in the area, were permanently tainted by the scandal. One of George's remaining children moved overseas; the other chose to stay in the family home until his death several years ago. He only had one son, Danc, who is the last of the once-great Crispin empire."

Keira chewed on the edge of her thumb. When she'd first seen Emma, she'd assumed the injuries had come from a spur-of-the-moment attack, such as a mugging, with the attacker fleeing the scene. Knowing that she'd been killed by the town's most prominent social figure made the situation both much simpler and much more complicated.

There was no need for her to uncover Emma's murderer because he'd already been found. Whatever Keira wanted to learn about him would probably be public knowledge. But he'd been caught, convicted, and incarcerated...so why did Emma's ghost linger?

"Keira?" Mason watched her closely while he scratched around the cat's head. The black creature's tongue had emerged again, and it showed no signs of retracting. "Do you remember something?"

"Ah, no, I'm afraid not. But it's a fascinating story." She rubbed at the back of her neck. "I was just thinking about Emma. And whether she'd have returned to town if she'd known George was capable of murder."

"Good question. I like to think so. Love can make people do reckless, crazy things."

The cat tried to roll onto its back but slipped off Mason's lap. He lunged to catch it, then chuckled as he set it onto the rug. "I'd better get going. As much as I'd like to stay longer, I promised to help my neighbor wash her dogs." He made a face. "She's a tiny woman pushing eighty with three Great Danes the size of horses. I'm seriously worried that one of them will sit on her and squash her someday."

Keira followed him to the door. "I'd better let you go to her rescue, then. Thanks for visiting. It was nice."

"It was, wasn't it?" He paused in the doorway. "I'll come back in a couple of days to take the stitches out. But give me a call if you need anything—even if you just want to chat. I have too much time on my hands these days."

Keira waved as he left, then she closed the door and went to the window. His long coat swirled around his legs as he strode through the graveyard, and the wind swept through his chocolate hair as he disappeared into the mist.

CHAPTER 13

MASON'S STORY HAD SOLVED the mystery of Emma's death, but it didn't answer why she remained on earth. Keira paced the length of the cottage, rubbing one hand over her mouth, as she thought it through.

Is it possible that Emma doesn't know her killer was caught? She's a ghost, but that doesn't mean she's omnipotent. Could she think George Crispin is still a free man?

It was worth a try. Keira crossed to the shopping bags and retrieved the bunch of daisies Polly Kennard had given her. The little black cat followed at her heels as she returned to the door, and Keira smiled at it. "Want to go outside for a bit?"

The cat gave a squeaky meow and butted at her leg. Keira opened the door, and it frisked out ahead of her, dancing through the barren garden as though it had lived there its entire life.

Mason's visit had consumed a lot of the morning. Keira

didn't have long until she needed to meet Zoe for coffee. She pulled her hoodie up over her head and passed into the graveyard.

The groundskeeper's garden had been neglected for a long time. Dead stems crunched under Keira's boots as she rounded the stone fence. According to Adage, the old groundskeeper had only passed a year before, but it seemed as though he'd been neglecting his duties for upward of a decade. Either that, or things just decayed faster in Blighty's cemetery. Keira scanned the markers and saw little recent intervention. There were very few flowers and no gifts, even though many of the stones had been placed within the past few years.

Something cold grazed her cheek and she shuddered, hiking her shoulders up. Nothing was visible, but the presences around her didn't want to be forgotten.

She turned toward the forest, retracing her path to the space where Emma's spirit had indicated to her grave. The paper around the daisies crinkled as she pressed them to her chest.

Mist dragged against her ankles like a current. She thought she heard a distant noise: a child crying. It was gone before she could even turn toward it. Keira swallowed, her tongue dry, and focused on the small, plain grave marker ahead. The name *Emma Carthage* seemed to rise out of the mist.

Keira paused ahead of the monument, staring at the block of dead grass that must have covered Emma and her casket, then she bent to place the daisies, propping them against the stone. As she stepped back, she wondered how many years it had been since anyone had left a gift for the weeping woman. Or if there had been any gifts left at all.

The daisies looked unnaturally fresh and bright against the neglected stone. It wasn't as old as many of its companions, but cracks had begun to form around the edge where frost had worked into the stone's weaknesses, and gray lichen clung to the surface. It was a sad monument. Lonely, like so many others in the graveyard. She cleared her throat. "Emma?"

There was no response, but she hadn't expected one.

"I hope you can hear me, Emma. I know who killed you. It was George Crispin, wasn't it?"

Again, she waited. The world seemed exceptionally quiet. Even though the forest edge was only two dozen paces away, she couldn't make out any noises from it. But something in the air seemed to change. It was only a tiny difference—a prickle of raised hairs, a breath of slightly cooler air—but Keira knew she wasn't alone.

"He was caught, Emma. Caught and convicted and spent fifteen years in prison. He died in there."

Mist rose from her lips with every word. The temperature was dropping; it stung her cheeks and chilled the inside of her nose. She took another step back from the gravestone but fought the impulse to retreat further. "He saw justice. You're free to move on, if you feel ready."

A muted crunching sound came from near her feet. The daisies under the headstone were withering. The petals turned black while the leaves darkened and shriveled. Even the blue-tinted paper holding them together seemed to age, curling as though from water damage while the color bleached out of it.

Keira still couldn't see anyone, but fog thickened between the headstones. The sky had been overcast all morning, but it deepened further into an angry black.

"Emma? Is this what you wanted? He was punished for his crime. I know it doesn't undo what happened, but—"

Frost spread outward from the dead flowers. The white crystals threaded up the headstone and spread over the grass, transforming it from brown to gray. Keira inched back from the ice's reach and wrapped her arms around her torso. She felt as if she'd fallen into a frozen lake.

Run, her instincts pleaded, but she still hesitated. She'd promised to help the ghost if she could, but her news seemed unwelcome. She couldn't understand it. Hadn't Emma wanted justice? Did she think prison was too light of a retribution?

Hearing a faint exhale, Keira turned. Behind her loomed a wall of fog. It was dense, suffocating. Keira tried to draw breath, and her lungs stung as frozen air hit them.

Black eyes stared out of the mist. Emma's beautiful face was contorted. Wild. The blood streaking down her cheek was no longer transparent monochrome but bright, violent red.

I can hear her breathing. I can see her color. What's happening?

The spirit's jaw stretched open. Behind the teeth was an endless pit of rotting flesh and squirming maggots, stretching away, as the throat shook with a howling scream. Keira pitched backward. Her legs hit the tombstone; she tumbled over it, gasped as she fell, and smashed into the dirt. Something—a rock or the corner of a gravestone, she wasn't sure—scraped the back of her shoulder. Red-hot pain pulsed through the shock.

Get up! Run!

The cold was all-consuming. Ice crystals flowed across Keira's skin as she scrambled to regain her feet. Emma reached toward her, her howling cry a deafening, unending tone that filled Keira's head and drowned out conscious thought. The outstretched hands hit Keira and passed through her. Cold burrowed into her chest, and she felt her heart miss a beat before stuttering back to life.

She couldn't tell if the spirit continued to scream or if the wails were merely trapped in her ears, destined to loop forever. She was blind in the impossibly thick mist. The freezing blanket of white pressed against her on all sides, so dense that she felt as if she were drowning in it. She couldn't see anything—not the spirit, the gravestones, or even the ground.

A tiny, muted meow came from somewhere to her right. Keira responded instinctively. She staggered toward it, holding her breath, simply hoping that she wouldn't collide with any of the hidden stones. Something dark flashed through the endless white. A cat's tail, its tip curled, bobbed like a lantern in the void, and Keira focused her remaining energy on following it.

The shape wove and flicked. It moved faster than Keira could have imagined; even at a full run, she only caught glimpses of the little black cat's twitching ears before it faded back into the fog.

Then, abruptly, the cat slowed to a trot, allowing Keira to catch up to it. A dark shape emerged from the drowning mist:

a familiar wooden door. The cat craned its head toward Keira, whiskers puffed and tail twitching, as it waited impatiently.

Keira felt emotionally numb as she turned the handle. She followed the cat inside the cottage and slammed the door. Suddenly, she could breathe again.

Her chest ached. She sucked in fresh oxygen as she pressed her back to the wood. The mist had drenched her and soaked through both layers of clothes; water dripped off her face and hair. She wiped the moisture away from her eyes and turned toward the window.

It was a cold but relatively clear day. The graveyard, dappled by muted sunlight, appeared peaceful. Keira swore under her breath.

The cat wove around her legs, rubbing itself against her jeans and purring so loudly that it sounded like a motor. Keira stared at it, then bent, picked it up, and cuddled it to her chest as she carried it to the empty fireplace.

This isn't just a regular cat, is it? She found me; she led me out of the mist. I don't know what would have happened if I'd been trapped out there, but I suspect I owe her an awful lot.

"You're wet," she murmured, and smudged some of the dew off the cat's head. It arched into her hand, purring gleefully, and Keira shuffled forward to light a fire.

As soon as the flames caught, she went to retrieve two towels from the bathroom. The first went to blotting as much water out of the cat as possible. She used the second to dry her hair, then pulled off the wet clothes and changed them for dry items from the bundle on the round table.

She glanced outside as she passed the window. The scene remained peaceful and clear. *The mist rose in minutes but disappeared in seconds. Almost as though the ghost had to work to manifest it but could only hold it for a short time.*

Keira fetched a new can of cat food from the bags, scraped it onto a plate, then cautiously approached her helper.

The cat had sprawled in front of the flames, its purrs now dulled to a low rumble, and showed no interest in the food she placed near it.

"Um…thank you." Keira tried not to feel stupid as she knelt beside the cat. "For helping me."

The cat twisted onto its back to expose maximum belly real estate to the heat. A smile pulled at Keira's mouth, but she fought to keep her voice gentle and polite. "Can you understand me? I'm assuming you're not a normal cat."

No response. After a second, Keira reached forward to scratch its chin. The feline redoubled its purrs, and its paws twitched.

Could it have been dumb luck? Is it possible she's just a normal cat after all?

"Well…if you can understand me…there's some food there. You're welcome to stay as long as you'd like. And, uh, thank you again."

The cat licked its nose but failed to retract its tongue. The little pink protrusion made it impossible for Keira to take the creature seriously. She chuckled as she brushed her hair out of her face. "Well, if you're planning to stay here much longer, I'm going to need to call you something. Got any suggestions?" The cat stretched luxuriously. "No? Then…how about…" The bunch of flowers below Emma's grave appeared in Keira's mind's eye. "How about Daisy? Is that all right?"

No answer. That either meant she approved, or she was just a normal, nonsapient cat who had no clue what Keira was saying. Either way… "Daisy it is."

Keira sat back and watched the flames. She was still shaking from the experience in the graveyard, but at least her heart had stopped fluttering like a panicked bird.

Emma seemed angry. More than angry…furious. So much so that she appeared more corporeal. Is it possible that ghosts' tangibleness is based on how strong their emotions are? When I saw her the first night, she was agitated. But none of the other ghosts were visible until I strained to see them. Is that because they're not distressed like Emma is?

Keira sighed and ran her hands over her face. "What upset her? It must have been something I said." She peeked through her fingers to watch the cat, who was happily ignoring the world. "D'you think George was wrongfully accused or something? Mason said he admitted to the crime, but what if he was covering up for someone, like one of his sons? That could explain Emma's frustration."

The cat's face twitched as it enjoyed the fire. Keira hoped it was having happy thoughts. She let her arms drop and leaned back. *I'll have to keep looking for answers. I don't think she meant to hurt me—it felt as though she was just so broken that she couldn't contain herself. Which means she must need the help badly. And I'm the only one who knows.*

She glanced at the clock on the fireplace mantel. It was nearly one.

"Oh no." Keira scrambled to her feet, startling the cat. "Sorry, Daisy, I've got to go. I promised I'd meet Zoe. I'll be back later, okay?"

The cat hiccupped, and its tongue poked out even farther.

Keira snorted as she ran to the door. *My life is a joke. Not only am I seeing dead people, but now I'm talking to my cat and actually expecting her to answer. If anyone saw me like this, they'd check me into a mental institution in a heartbeat.*

She looked through the window a final time. The idea of leaving her cottage's relative safety wasn't appealing, but the cemetery appeared calm. A family had arrived to pay their respects to a grave near the opposite fence. Keira took a fortifying breath, slipped through the door, and turned toward town. She was going to be late for her meeting with Zoe, and there would be hell to pay.

CHAPTER 14

ZOE STOOD OUTSIDE THE café, her arms crossed and her face a mask of pure disgust. "Keira Jane Doe. Do you know how long I've been waiting?"

"Sorry!" Keira slowed to a halt and pressed a hand to her torso. She'd run from the church, and not even her muscles could save her from breathlessness.

"I've been here for *at least* four minutes. That's, like, equivalent to an entire month of a mayfly's life."

"What?"

"Never mind. Get your butt in that café; we're going to have to hustle to catch up to our schedule."

"We have a schedule?"

Instead of answering, Zoe planted her hands on Keira's back and shoved her inside the shop. "Grab the corner table before any of the plebeians steal it. Whatcha want? Another hot chocolate? Too bad if not, because I already ordered it."

Keira gave up on trying to follow the flow of words and allowed Zoe to push her toward the same corner they'd shared the day before. As she sank into the plush armchair, she scanned the café. It was busy. An older couple laughed together at the next table over. Five gray-haired women had co-opted the largest table and were happily talking over each other. A queue was forming at the counter as Zoe got into an argument with the sallow barista. Unlike the day before, Keira no longer felt anxious.

I'm starting to put down roots, she realized with a jolt. *I'm creating friendships, thinking of certain café seats as "mine," feeling responsibility over the fate of a restless spirit... This isn't good. Chances are I'll need to leave soon, and it will be heartbreaking to say goodbye.*

"Okay." Zoe collapsed into the seat opposite. "Firstly, Marlene is an awful person for not letting me order a mug of pure caramel syrup." She raised her voice to holler across the crowded café. "It's a free country, Marlene!"

Marlene, the barista, yelled back, "I refuse to let my tax dollars pay for the heart transplant you'll eventually need!"

"Whatever," Zoe grumbled. She leaned over and opened her bag. "Secondly, if we're going to work on this mystery together—"

"We are?"

"Shush. No objections. If we're going to work together, you'll need this."

Zoe slid a small mobile phone across the table. The sight reminded Keira of the bags of groceries sitting in the cottage's kitchen. She'd intended to return them to Zoe, but the shock of the graveside encounter had chased it out of her mind. She held up both hands, refusing to touch the phone. "Thanks, but I don't need charity."

"It's not charity, moron." Zoe rolled her eyes. "It's for strategic planning and coordinating. Pretend you're James Bond and I'm what's his face who gives Bond his awesome gadgets."

Keira raised a skeptical eyebrow at the phone. It was a flip model that looked at least a decade old. "MI6 had some budget cuts."

"Shush, you."

Marlene, balancing an armful of plates, arrived at the table. She gave Zoe one very long, very sour glare, then placed three dishes and two cups in front of them. "One hot chocolate for the polite lady who deserves better company. And enough calories to kill a hippo for the problematic one."

"Love you too, Marlene," Zoe retorted, waving her off.

"I forgot this was your lunch break. You must be hungry," Keira said, eyeing the pancakes and bowl of nachos.

Zoe nudged a fork toward her. "Yeah, I kinda got carried away. Help me finish some of this, will ya?"

Ah. Keira leaned back in her chair and folded her arms. *I should've guessed.* "Thanks, but like I said, I don't need charity."

Zoe's owl eyes widened into the perfect image of innocence. "It's not. You'd be doing me a favor. I'd feel horribly wasteful if I didn't finish this food. Think of the hungry kids in other countries or whatever."

"I'm not just talking about this. I found the canned foods hidden in the cat supplies."

"What, really? Wow, they must have accidentally fallen in by accident or something. Whoops. No returns."

Keira wanted to frown, but Zoe was too ridiculous to let her create the right facial shape. Instead, she made sure her voice was firm. "I appreciate that you're trying to do a good deed or whatever, but I'll buy my own food."

"Well, I was *trying* to be discreet about it." Zoe sighed and let her head loll back in exaggerated frustration. "But c'mon. I gave you the benefit of the doubt yesterday, thinking maybe you just really, really liked rice, but then you had to admit this morning that you couldn't afford a can of cat food. I *don't* let my friends starve."

Keira tried to come up with a retort, but the best she could manage was "Who said we're friends?"

"I did, idiot. Eat the damn food."

Pride tried to argue. The food was charity, and that made her an inconvenient liability. The tally of people Keira intended to one day pay back was growing rapidly, but she knew Zoe was right. *The day you can't buy cat food is the day to get over your ego and accept some help.* She picked up the fork and cut a corner off the pancake. "So the mobile phone's for coordinating secret meetings and getaway cars, right?"

Animation flooded back into Zoe's face. "Oh, yeah! And the best thing—the government doesn't know about it. It's prepaid. I bought it in the city while wearing a fake mustache, then removed any parts that could be used for tracking. There's absolutely no way to trace it back to us."

"That's a joke, right?"

Zoe snorted. "Please. It's important to ensure all aspects of your life are as anonymous as possible. Anyone who's still on the grid when the machines reach sentience is going to have a really, really bad day."

"Of course." Keira had a lot she wanted say to that but swallowed it. "Thanks."

Zoe looked genuinely pleased. "Anytime. Ready to go through some of my theories?"

"Absolutely."

A folder came out of the bag. Zoe managed to squeeze it between the plates and began leafing through. Keira peeked at the turning pages and saw a bizarre mix of arcane symbols, Illuminati eyes, a language that looked suspiciously like Elvish, a map of Madagascar, and blurry photos of what were presumably flying saucers.

"I was up researching most of the night," Zoe said, pausing to linger over a lovingly rendered depiction of a Lovecraftian monstrosity. "To be fair, though, that describes most of my nights. But I researched extra hard last night and have some pretty compelling theories. How much do you know about the freemasons?"

"Oh, it's Mason."

Zoe frowned. "No. Freemasons. The organization that may or may not be responsible for the chemtrails over Portugal last year."

"No, I mean Mason—he's here." Keira craned to see through the crowd. Mason had come through the café's door and was placing his order with Marlene.

"Aw crap!" Zoe shot a glance toward the counter, then grabbed the top of Keira's head and tried to force her down. "Okay, he's definitely stalking you. Hide under the table. I'll distract him while you make your escape."

"Ow, please, cut that out. He's obviously here to have lunch." Keira had underestimated Zoe's strength and had to fight to stay above the table.

The commotion caught Mason's attention, and a smile brightened his face as he saw them. He passed several notes to Marlene, motioning for her to keep the change, and began to make his way toward their table.

"Damn it!" Zoe snapped forward again, her eyes as round as saucers. "Okay. This is okay. Play it cool, Keira. Don't let him know we suspect him."

"Keira! It's good to see you in town. You've met Zoe, I see."

Zoe shot him a glare that would have melted steel beams. "Keep your grubby hands off my friend, murderer."

So much for playing it cool. Keira wished she'd sunk under the table after all. She opened her mouth to apologize to Mason, but the English language didn't even contain half the words she needed to express what she felt.

To her surprise, Mason appeared unfazed. He beamed at Zoe. "Murderer? Please, I'm not a fool. No one in town can string together evidence like you. If I were in the habit of killing people, there's no way I would have let you live long enough to incriminate me."

Zoe was silent for a moment as she chewed on the inside of

her cheek. Then she nodded as though the situation had been resolved and patted Keira's arm. "He makes a good point. It's probably safe to trust him again."

Mason bent closer to Keira, his expression perfectly serious. "Or is it?" He winked. "Would the pair of you like any company for lunch?"

Zoe shrugged. "We're going through theories for how Keira ended up here. Find yourself a seat and try not to sound as ignorant as you are, ignoramus."

Again heat rose across Keira's face. She considered kicking Zoe under the table, but then a warm hand landed on her shoulder.

Keira met Mason's sparkling green eyes, and he gave her arm a reassuring squeeze. "Don't worry. Zoe and I went to school together. I'm used to her." He slid a spare seat up to Keira's side of the table. It wasn't a spacious area, and Keira tried not to feel too conscious of how their elbows brushed when he sat down.

"And I'm used to you in the same way that a person gets used to an ax in their head," Zoe retorted. "Bloody traitorous capitalistic sellout."

"She doesn't like that I chose to study medicine," Mason explained. "It's too mainstream for her taste."

"You may as well have signed up for a class on brainwashing. All they do is spoon-feed you institutionalized lies and teach you how to perpetuate Big Pharma's monopoly on human suffering."

He nodded gravely. "The whole business of saving lives is exceptionally corrupt. The world would have been a better place if I'd studied UFO phenomena instead."

Zoe snatched the folder off the table and hefted it, as though threatening to beat him with it. "Behave, plague monger, or I'll evict you from the meeting."

"All right, understood! I'll be good." He folded his arms on the table and leaned forward, but Keira noticed his shoulders were twitching from repressed laughter. "What have you come up with?"

Zoe slammed the folder back onto the table and took a deep breath. "Well, the best lead we've got right now is the men who were following her. They didn't match the descriptions or modus operandi of any of the better-known secret organizations, but they could be a local group. Or a group that's so secret, we don't even know they exist. Isn't that an awful idea? The world could be full of societies so covert that we never hear of them." Zoe made a face. "Ghastly."

Keira shrugged. "Adage spoke to one of them. He might be able to describe him, but that won't help much unless they return."

"Wait." Mason's smile disappeared as he turned to Keira. "I thought she was joking. Was someone following you?"

Ah, that's right—I didn't tell him what happened, and it looks like Adage hasn't either. "Sorry. I thought you knew—"

"Adage only told me you'd arrived in town without any memories. What happened, Keira?"

All joviality had dropped from his expression. His intense green eyes flicked to the hidden cut on her shoulder before locking back on to her face. She knew he must be building up a plethora of possible scenarios, just as she had.

Keira recounted her first night in Blighty as coherently as she could. Zoe, who had already heard the story, returned to leafing through her folder, but Mason's attention didn't waver.

When she'd finished, he frowned at the table as he ran his hand over his mouth. "That's serious. Have you been to the police about it?"

"No, and I don't intend to." Keira threaded her hands together, the knuckles white. "There's the possibility that I could have done something illegal before I lost my memories. And…and I don't want to go to prison for it."

He nodded slowly.

"Besides." Zoe tore off a strip of pancake and stuffed it into her mouth. "Blighty's police are equal amounts incompetent and corrupt. She's better off not drawing attention to herself."

"I don't know about corrupt, but it's true it's been a few years since Constable Sanderson cared about his job." Mason lapsed into thought again and only broke out of it when Marlene arrived at the table with his food. "Thanks, Marl. You haven't heard news of any new blood coming through town, have you?"

She dipped her head toward Keira. "Other than this one? Nah."

Mason nodded as the woman returned to her counter. "News travels fast in this town, and Has Beans is the most popular watering hole for sharing it. If Marlene hasn't heard of strangers staying in or visiting Blighty, they're either gone or being extremely stealthy."

"If they only come out at night, it would support my leading theory." Zoe held up the binder. "*Vampires.*"

Mason turned back to Keira. "I'm not sure the cemetery's cottage is the best place to stay. It's too far from town and backs right onto the forest."

She shrugged. "That makes it a pretty good hiding place in my book. Anyone who's new to Blighty probably won't know it's there."

"True. But I'd still feel more comfortable if you were closer to the town's center." He hesitated. "Or in another town altogether."

Zoe flicked a blueberry in Mason's direction. "Good thing your comfort isn't her priority, huh?"

Keira, sensing an argument brewing, leaned in. "I actually like the isolation. If anyone's still looking for me, they're likely to focus their efforts where the most people are—in Blighty's center. Adage offered to help me relocate to another area, but…" *I'm putting down roots. I have friends here. I like this town.* "The plan right now is to stay in Blighty. For the short term, at least."

He smiled. "I can see you've thought this through."

Is it my imagination, or does he look relieved? She picked up her fork and focused on demolishing her half of the pancakes. "It's a risk to stay here, but there'll be risks no matter where I go."

"You can reduce that by having some means of contacting help. The cottage doesn't have a phone, does it?"

"Already sorted." Zoe nudged the flip phone on the table.

Mason nodded. "Good. May I?" He opened the mobile, spent a moment pressing buttons, then passed it back to Keira. "I put my number in there. Call me if there's any trouble. I don't get out of Blighty much, so I'll never be more than five minutes away. I also added Constable Sanderson's personal cell phone. He doesn't answer the station's phone after five, but he'll pick up that number even if it's the middle of the night. Okay?"

"Great, thank you." She tucked it into her pocket. "And if all else fails, I have a ferocious guard cat."

"Mm." Zoe waved her fork while she struggled to swallow a mouthful of food. "The vet nurse came through my checkout this morning. She knows, like, every single animal in this town, so I asked her, but she says the only black cats around here have white markings or are fat. Yours must've come from another town."

"It would be a long way to travel," Mason said. "What do you think you'll do with her?"

"Uh…" That was hard to answer. Keira very dearly wanted to keep the black creature, but the situation was a minefield of question marks. If she couldn't get a job, she wouldn't be able to feed it. And most landlords prohibited pets. "Good question."

Zoe flapped her folder at them. "Are we ready to get back to the serious stuff or what? My lunch break ends soon."

"Right, the serious stuff, of course." The flicker of humor had returned to Mason's eyes, though he did a good job of maintaining a solemn face as he folded his hands on the table. "Vampires, was it?"

"Oh, ye of little faith." Zoe opened her folder to a page filled with illustrations, including a medley of traditional Dracula-inspired horrors alongside naked, animalistic creatures. "Popular media has turned vampires into a joke, but there's still plenty of evidence for their existence. A whole bunch of different cultures have folklore about bloodsucking monsters. And the descriptions—pallid faces, only seen at night, inaudible movement—line up nicely with the figure I saw outside my window."

Keira rubbed at the back of her neck. "Look, it's not that I'm not grateful for this, but…vampires? Really?"

"They'd need somewhere to hide during daylight hours." Mason seemed to be having far too much fun. "So that they don't burn to dust, y'know."

Zoe seemed to take his comment seriously as she nodded. "Course. And where better than the home of our resident vampire: Ol' Crispy?"

Mason inclined his head toward Keira. "She means Dane Crispin. His house is…ah…old-fashioned, and it invites a lot of rumors."

"Calling it old-fashioned is like saying the queen is a little bit fancy. The thing's basically a gothic mansion."

Keira glanced between the two of them. It seemed incredible that the subject of her most pressing concern—Emma's death—would crop up by chance. She tried to keep her voice casual. "I'm not going to pretend I'm an expert on this town or anything…but I've been here three days without seeing any kind of mansion."

"It's mostly hidden by the forest," Mason said, "but it's only a few minutes from here. It's a stunning building—I could take you there one day, if you're interested."

"Yes!" Keira knew she probably sounded too eager, but she didn't care. "How about now?"

Mason laughed. "Now? All right, I'm game. Let's go."

"But—but—" Zoe huffed a sigh. "Jeez. I was meant to be back at work five minutes ago, and we didn't even touch on my secondary theory involving the Zodiac Killer. Hang on a minute."

She pulled out her phone, dialed a number, and waited for it to ring. "Hey, Lucas, it's Zoe. Cover my shift at the grocery store, okay? Yes, I know. If you *had* a job I wouldn't do this to you. Stop complaining. You got plenty of practice yesterday." She hung up the phone, slipped it into her pocket, and returned the folder to her bag. The manic light brightened her owl-like eyes. "All right, time to go hunt a vampire."

CHAPTER 15

KEIRA FOLLOWED MASON AND Zoe back onto the main street. They led her toward the half of the town she hadn't yet seen. Mason matched her pace and shared some of what he knew while Zoe loped ahead.

"Dane was born a few years after Emma's murder and George's incarceration, but he's unfortunately been tainted by the association. As far as I know, the only person he's on close terms with is Dr. Kelsey. Apparently, the families were friendly, and George paid for the doctor's studies, so Kelsey continues to stay in touch with the grandson. Dane doesn't leave Crispin House often, though I've heard some people have seen him wandering the streets at night, which is the basis for Zoe's delightful vampire theory."

"Is he a nice person?"

"I don't know him well. Some people say he's haughty and

antisocial. I'm more inclined to think he struggles with anxiety and possibly a persecution complex because of what his grandfather did." Mason pulled a face. "Some people in this town go to great lengths to make sure he doesn't forget it."

"Why doesn't he move?"

"I'm not sure. It might be from family loyalty, fear of the unknown, or it's possible he even likes the attention. Like I said, I don't know him—the only time I see him is during the town meetings."

"Oy!" Zoe turned so that she was walking backward and waved her arms. "If you're going to natter away like a pair of old women, at least have the decency to talk about the interesting stuff. I heard Ol' Crispy planted a tree in the place where his grandpa tried to bury Carthage. Like some sort of twisted monument."

"That's a rumor that has been floating around for years." Mason put his hands in his jacket pockets and shrugged. "I'd be surprised if it were true."

They were leaving the town's center and passing through the residential areas. The farther they walked, the more rural the properties appeared. The houses closest to the main street had tidy suburban lawns, but farther out, they morphed into hobby farms and sprawling properties.

"The Crispin House is just through here." Mason indicated what looked like the edge of the forest. "It used to be more open, but the Crispins planted the trees shortly after the scandal to help preserve their privacy."

"Not that it helped much," Zoe called over her shoulder. "They got dragged through the mud big time. Can you imagine? George Crispin, the guy who thought his family was so much better than the dirty peasants in town, murdered a local girl in a fit of rage. The newspapers had a field day."

"And they're certain George was the killer?"

Mason quirked his head to the side. "I suppose so. Who else would it be?"

"Yeah, of course." Keira could feel him watching her. She ran her fingers through her hair so that some of it shifted forward to obscure her face.

She hadn't meant to voice her pet theory so openly, but it was striking her as increasingly strange that George Crispin, a cultured, respected man, would murder a girl from a poor family, then do such a poor job of hiding his crime.

But if it wasn't George, who did it? Surely not Frank. But perhaps one of George's other sons was motivated by jealousy, or even one of the staff—though I can't imagine George would take the fall for a staff member.

"Here we are." Mason had stopped in front of a fence that was dense with ivy. He pulled back a swath of the vine to expose a wrought-iron gate, then gestured for Keira to step up.

She did and peered through two metal bars. The aging, dilapidated building at the end of the driveway was everything she'd been promised and more.

Zoe had called it a mansion, and it was very close to being one. The three-story stone building crouched like a sleeping monster on the overgrown lawn. The windows were black and lifeless, and patches of the roof were collapsing.

"It's beautiful," Keira murmured.

"Figures you'd say that."

Keira glanced to her right and saw Zoe's face poking through the gate. "You think Blighty is cute too. No offense, but whatever lost your memories probably also screwed up your judgment skills."

Keira laughed and turned back to the manor. "No, it really is beautiful…in a melancholic sort of way. It must be too big for one person to clean and manage, but Dane doesn't have any staff, does he?"

"None," Mason said. "It wasn't exactly tipped to win home of the year when I was a child, but at least the roof was intact. He's not repairing it himself, though, and hasn't hired anyone. The rain must have ruined the rooms on that side of the building by now." He made a frustrated little noise. "Mold won't do his lungs any favors."

Longing filled Zoe's voice. "Think about all the awful secrets he could be hiding in there. What I wouldn't give to spend a night in Crispin House."

A neglected garden surrounded the house's front, and its unruly bushes pushed against the stone foundation. Keira licked her lips and hoped her question wasn't too morbid. "Is this where Emma was killed?"

"Nah," Zoe said. "He got her behind the house. She'd walked through the forest, probably by way of the mill, and met him in the backyard. This fence only surrounds three sides of the house, y'see? They used the woods to create a natural fourth wall."

Keira knew it was ridiculous to feel frustrated, but she'd hoped to see the scene of Emma's murder. What she expected to find there, she didn't know, but it was hard not to picture a half-dug grave in the middle of the vegetable garden, even though it certainly no longer existed.

"Imagine if he'd succeeded," Zoe breathed. "In hiding her body, I mean. If the groundskeeper hadn't seen Emma coming out of the woods and run to the police, George could have buried her without anyone knowing. No one heard from Emma's parents, even though the police requested they come forward. She would have just…disappeared off the face of the planet. No one would have known what happened to her except for George. And he'd have grown a squash plant over her grave, probably, so that the roots would absorb her body's nutrients, and every summer, Frank Crispin would have eaten a tiny bit of his beloved in the squash soup."

Mason sighed. "You're terrible, Zo."

Keira was only half listening. Something moved through the topiary off to one side of the house. A figure emerged from between two trees. She tugged on Zoe's sleeve and lowered her voice to a whisper, even though the figure was too far away to hear them. "Is that Dane?"

"Sure is," Zoe said. "Wanna call him over?"

"No." Keira and Mason spoke in unison.

Mason continued. "It's hard enough for him with the way

some people in the town gossip. I don't want him to think his house is part of an unofficial tour or anything."

"Jeez, relax. This is a public road. There aren't any rules against looking at a house."

Keira knew she should move back from the fence but found it impossible to look away from the strange man. He was tall and spindly but hunched in a way that significantly disguised it. His clothes were well worn, and long, greasy hair hung around his neck. Stubble covered sunken cheeks, and creases around his mouth and eyes framed a permanent scowl. He looked almost like a reflection of his house: uncared for and grimly resentful.

Dane's head suddenly snapped in their direction. Keira jumped back from the fence, letting the vines fall back into place and tugging Zoe back alongside her.

"Aw, c'mon," Zoe protested. "I wanted to see what he'd do."

"Mason's right. We shouldn't gawk." Embarrassment was creeping over Keira. She could only hope Dane hadn't seen them. *Mercy knows I don't like people staring at me, and I'm not even trying to hide from my family's history.* "Sorry," she said to Mason. "I shouldn't have asked you to bring me here."

He still wore his characteristically cheerful smile. "Don't feel too bad. Plenty of people come to look at the house—it's just not very common to also see Dane."

Zoe planted her hands on her hips and gave a mischievous grin. "Seeing as we're already so close, what say we take a look at the mill? I haven't been up this way in a while, and I want to see if it's collapsed yet."

"Don't you need to get back to the store?" Keira looked down the road that led toward the town.

"Pshaw. Lucas will watch it. It's about time he got a real job anyway."

Keira looked at Mason, who smiled. "I'm game if you are."

"All right. Let's go."

CHAPTER 16

ONCE AGAIN, ZOE LED the way, maintaining a blistering pace and occasionally stopping to wait for her companions to catch up. Keira and Mason followed at a slower speed. Keira couldn't stop herself from glancing at the ivy-coated fence that ran parallel to the path, but she didn't catch any other glimpses of the house. At one point, she heard the faint rustle of vegetation and turned just in time to see the vines fall still. It was hard not to imagine Dane on the other side of the fence, watching them in the same way they'd watched him.

The dirt path took a sharp turn to the right as they passed the edge of the Crispin property, and the trees thinned to reveal untended pastures and infrequent farmhouses. A huge, dark building dominated one of the fields.

"Is that—"

"Yep," Zoe said, glee evident in her voice. "Old Crispin Mill.

No one wants to spend the money to pull it down—especially as the land isn't worth much—so they're just letting it sit there until it falls apart on its own."

That might take a while. The brick building was certainly old, and time had eroded some parts, but the structure had clearly been designed to last. Even if the roof collapsed, Keira imagined the walls could easily stand for another hundred years.

They left the dirt road to approach the building. The grass grew past Keira's thighs, but dozens of footsteps, likely from equally curious visitors, had created a winding pathway through the tall weeds.

The structure was vast. Its windows were small and infrequent, and the roof blotted out a great swath of sky. In its day, it would have been large enough to hold several hundred workers.

As she neared the building, a prickly sensation touched Keira's back. She shifted her shoulder blades to rub it away, but it didn't leave. It was a soft force—almost undetectable—but made her uneasy. She'd felt it before, while standing in her graveyard as the mist rolled over the tombstones.

Death has tainted this ground, her subconscious whispered. *Blood was spilled here.*

She slowed. Peering through the web-crusted windows no longer seemed like a good idea.

"Keira?" Mason came to a halt a step ahead of her. "Are you okay?"

Her mouth was dry. "Yeah. It's just…uh…"

She tilted her head back to see up the height of the building.

Its roof towered high above her, and the bricks were stained by streaks of sooty discoloration marking where decades of water had flowed. The building was hostile. Bitter. *Dangerous.*

This was a cruel place to work. Trapped inside, with so few windows, the high roof making you feel like you could be crushed any second. And the deaths…so many of them…accidents…machinery malfunctions…suicides…

"Keira." Mason's hand came to rest on her back, bracing her. "You're white as a sheet. Did something happen? Do you feel sick?"

She shook herself. A high-pitched ringing noise filled her head and made her dizzy. "Huh?"

"C'mon. Let's get you away from here." He tried to guide her back from the building, but she held her ground. Her head was clearing. The looming, prickling sense of unease had retreated into the background of her awareness. Mason stood close, his hand still on her back, his sharp green eyes skipping over her face. Zoe stood next to one of the windows, watching. Neither seemed affected by the building the way Keira had been.

She managed a laugh, but it felt dead in her ears. "Sorry, I kinda spaced out for a moment there. I'm fine."

The worried creases around Mason's eyes told her he didn't believe it. "You don't look well. Let's go back to the road."

Keira opened her mouth to object, but before she could, Zoe skipped forward and looped an arm through Keira's. Unlike Mason's worried frown, Zoe's expression was cheerful and easy. "It's an ugly building anyway. I doubt even *you* could say something complimentary about it. Let's go back to town; I want an ice cream."

With Zoe refusing to let go of her left arm and Mason's gentle, guiding hand on her right shoulder, Keira let herself be led back toward the dirt road. It only took a dozen steps for the prickling sensation to slip away from her, and she began to feel that she could lower her guard again.

Zoe maintained an animated, one-sided conversation the entire walk back to the road. Before long, Keira realized the subjects—which ranged from JFK's assassination to local sightings of an albino panther—were intended to distract her from the building behind them. She squeezed Zoe's arm to let the other woman know she was okay. "Thanks, Zo. You can stop talking now."

Zoe stuck her tongue out. "Who says I want to?"

They'd reached the road. The town's rooftops silhouetted against the afternoon horizon seemed farther away than Keira had thought they'd walked.

Mason rubbed at the back of his neck. "Would you like to sit down for a moment? There's a fallen tree—"

"Jeez, no. I'm fine. Honestly." This time, her laugh was genuine. She unthreaded her arm from Zoe's and began striding toward town. "I just…got a bit dazed."

"You looked frightened." Mason allowed her to duck out from under his hand but stayed near her. "Did the mill remind you of something?"

She fought the temptation to glance over her shoulder at the building. "Maybe. I'm not sure. It wasn't a memory. More like… the memory of an emotion." *Other people's emotions. Pain, misery, suffering…death.* She pushed her hands into her jeans pockets to disguise a shudder.

Zoe swung her arms as she stepped around a patch of potholes. "Like I said, it's an ass-ugly building. Not really interesting either, just a bunch of abandoned junk. Rebellious kids sometimes visit it at night and tell ghost stories."

"Ha, yes, my friends and I used to do that. First to leave was branded a chicken." Mason snorted. "Looking back on it, it's a miracle none of us stepped on any of the rusty metal and got tetanus."

"Huh," Zoe said. "I thought it would be impossible to paint an abandoned mill in a boring light, but look at you go."

His face scrunched up with the smile he beamed back at her. "Believe me, there's nothing boring about tetanus or any of the other endospores. They can remain dormant for centuries—"

"Okay, now I *have* to know. Are you naturally this awful, or do you put in special effort?"

Keira had to chuckle. The farther they walked from the mill, the more human she felt, and Zoe and Mason's bickering faded into the background as Keira examined what had happened.

Apparently, my abilities aren't limited to seeing ghosts. I seem to pick up on…I don't know what to call them. Emotional imprints? The ghosts of memories? It's like death stained the mill, and I can see it.

She suspected there would have been a lot more to see if she'd looked through the window.

They reentered the main street and turned toward the center fountain. They hadn't quite reached it when the general store's door was thrown open and a miserable, disheveled teen poked his head out and wailed, "Zo-*e*!"

Zoe exhaled a long-suffering sigh. "Looks like I won't be getting that ice cream. Take care of yourself, Keira. Later, nerd."

They waved as Zoe jogged toward Lucas, who was nearly in tears.

"Poor kid," Keira muttered, and Mason laughed.

"I don't feel too sorry for him. He egged Zoe's house a few months back, so now his mother makes him do Zoe favors or else he's grounded."

"Ha! Gossip really does spread in this town." Keira could feel Mason watching her, so she made a show of stretching as though they'd done nothing more than go on a relaxing walk. "I should probably head home. Or, uh, back to the cottage at least."

"I'll walk with you," Mason offered.

She snorted. "I'm fine. Really. You can go home."

He folded his arms and bent over so they were at the same eye level, and a hint of amusement twitched at the corners of his mouth. "I never thought I'd quote Zoe, but who says I want to? It's a lovely day. I wouldn't mind enjoying a bit more of it before the sun sets."

"You call this lovely? It's been overcast the entire time."

"A day doesn't have to be sunny to be nice."

She raised an eyebrow. He grinned back.

"All right, you win." Keira stepped up beside him, and together they turned down the road that led toward the cemetery.

Mason seemed happy to walk in silence. He set a leisurely pace, and his eyes roved over the trees and the shrubs lining the path.

Keira found it hard not to watch him. "This must have been a weird day for you. All you wanted was lunch, but you ended up wandering all over the countryside."

"I don't get out as often as I should, so I enjoyed this."

"Good." She didn't know how well her next question would be received, so she phrased it carefully. "Zoe said you're taking a break from med school."

"Normally, I'd advise against taking Zoe's word on anything. But in this case, she's absolutely right."

He still seemed happy, so Keira risked pushing a little more. "Will you be going back?"

"Maybe." He shrugged. "We'll see."

"If you don't mind me asking, what made you leave?"

He glanced at her, and something dark clouded his eyes. Then he blinked, and the expression was replaced with the warm smile she was growing so fond of. "I lost my way. I chose to study medicine for a very specific reason, but one day, I realized that the original motivation was no longer driving me. Instead, I was making sacrifices for goals I'd never wanted— never *should* have wanted—and…I decided I needed to get out. Center myself. Figure out who I am." He laughed again, and it almost sounded natural. "I sound like a motivational poster right now, don't I?"

"One of the extra-cheesy ones," she replied, agreeing. "One with dolphins jumping over a sunset."

They were passing the parsonage. Adage was home; the lights were on and a disco track was floating through the open windows. "Thanks for walking me back."

"Anytime." Mason stopped and tilted his head to the side. He looked relaxed, but his expression held something strange. "Keira?"

"Yeah?"

He hesitated, then said, "Be safe, okay?"

"Of course I will."

He opened his mouth, closed it again, cleared his throat, and took a step back. "You have my number if you need anything. I'll see you soon."

"Good night."

She watched him start down the driveway, then turned toward her cottage. The sun was edging toward the horizon, and Keira tried not to shiver as she wove between the tombstones.

I didn't say anything to upset him, did I? She exhaled heavily and turned in to the cottage's dead garden. Zoe might be misguided about many topics, but Keira thought she'd identified something in Mason. He was discontent, and trying very hard to hide it. She just wished she understood why.

A piece of paper had been taped to the front door. Keira slowed as she neared it and recognized Adage's scrawl.

Keira,

I cooked a pie that I have no hope of finishing on my own. Would you care to join me for dinner?

Adage

Keira snorted and shook her head as she entered the cottage. *People around here are too nice.*

Daisy's large, amber eyes glowed from the kitchen. Keira turned on the cottage's light and found the scrawny, black cat sitting in the sink.

"What're you doing there?" She grinned as she carefully lifted the cat and moved her to the rug in front of the cooling fireplace. Daisy pushed her head against Keira's hand, so she gave the fuzzy ears a scratch. "You'll need to have dinner by yourself. I'm sorry. I hope you're not getting too lonely."

Daisy flopped onto her back and stretched out, paws poking toward the ceiling. Keira returned to the kitchen and served up a fresh can of cat food. She left it beside her companion, who ignored it except for a twitch of the nose. Keira gave the cat's head a final scratch before turning toward the door.

Visiting the Crispin properties didn't lend much to help me solve my ghost's problem, but I'm not out of options yet. Every town has its gossips, and I have a feeling Adage might be one of Blighty's.

CHAPTER 17

"COME IN, CHILD!" ADAGE'S voice echoed from inside.

Keira let herself through the open door and went in search of him. The house smelled like garlic and parsley, and Keira found the pastor surrounded by dirty pots in the kitchen. She grinned. "You've been busy."

"It always seems a waste to cook just for myself," Adage said as he pried the pie out of its tin. "But I really do love food, so I tend to go all out when I have a guest. If the Lord hadn't called me to his ministry, I think I should have liked to be a chef."

Keira took the empty pie tin from Adage and began stacking the mess by the sink so it didn't take up so much counter space. "Why not do both? Become a TV chef who recites sermons while preparing food. Call it the Cooking Church."

"I could see that working. 'Add a pinch of salt, just as you are to be the salt of the earth.' And then I could recommend accompanying communion wines."

"You're onto something now."

They laughed as they carried the food into the little dining alcove. Pots of herbs lined the ledge above the corner. Adage had already set out cutlery, so Keira sat at the wooden table while he served her.

"You've been busy today," he said, dropping a gigantic slice of pie onto her plate. "I came by twice, but you were out both times. I was afraid you might have moved on without saying goodbye."

"Never," she promised. "I met up with Zoe and Mason in town. They offered to show me around." It was the perfect segue, so she continued, "They took me to Dane Crispin's home and the old mill. I had no idea the town had such a rich history."

Adage poured them both water before he sat and steepled his fingers. "I think you'll find this area is full of little dramas and secrets. Do you mind if we say grace?"

Keira bowed her head while Adage said a few words. Once he finished, she straightened, trying to come up with a natural way to bring the conversation back to the mystery, but Adage spared her the trouble.

"I suppose they told you about poor Emma Carthage and Frank Crispin?"

"Yes. It must have been a shock for the town."

Adage speared a piece of broccoli as he shook his head. "It was terrible. I had only taken over the parsonage a year before their deaths, and I was so clueless. I'd given them counseling, you see, and it was hard not to think that perhaps I could have saved them if I'd known what was coming. It took a long time to learn how to forgive myself."

Keira froze with a piece of pie held near her mouth. "I didn't realize you knew them."

"Oh, yes. I wasn't much older than them, but they had asked me to officiate their secret wedding. It was to be a very quiet affair, held in the church after dark, with only the two of them and a couple of close friends in attendance. Emma and I waited at the church for hours, but Frank never showed. I didn't learn until the following morning that his father had locked him in his room. And, of course, while Emma was with me at the church, George Crispin went to her parents to negotiate the lovers' separation. The next time I saw Emma after that night was when she lay in her coffin." He shook his head. "It was a dark time, my dear. I confess I doubted the Lord's mercy that he would allow two such kind people to perish when they had been so close to happiness."

Keira had lost her appetite. She put her fork back on the plate. "I'm so sorry."

Adage shrugged. "I have grown since that time. I still regret what happened to Emma and Frank, but I have no doubt they met in the afterlife, where there can be no petty judgment or selfishness or suffering to separate them."

Keira glanced toward the window. Night had fallen, and the mist was already rolling in. She had to clench her hands to keep them from trembling. *Emma has not moved on. Is it possible that Frank lingers too? Does she live on this earth because she doesn't want to step into the next life without him?* "It sounds like they were deeply in love."

"Oh, yes, in the way two young, willful people tend to be." Adage had cheered a little and ate his meal with enthusiasm. "It was a very Romeo-and-Juliet situation, complete with warring families and a tragic ending. Don't you like the pie, my dear?"

"Ah, it's delicious!" Keira picked her fork up again, but her stomach was still too unsettled to let her eat, so she poked at her food while she chose her next question. "I suppose you must have known George Crispin as well?"

"Not closely. He had attended my predecessor's sermons but seemed to think I was too young to be at the pulpit, so only came at Christmas and Easter."

"It must have been a surprise to learn he was capable of murder, though." Keira was trying to prod around her theory that George hadn't been the killer, but it was impossible to say so outright without it sounding as though Zoe's conspiracy mania had rubbed off on her.

"Yes and no. He was an important member of our society, of course, and no one expects their neighbor to take a life. But during the trial, many witnesses came forward to speak of his violent nature. Business partners claimed to have been threatened. Staff reported physical violence. Many were of the opinion that he was a bomb waiting to go off and that Emma's reappearance pushed him an inch too far."

Damn. Keira tried another tack. "But Emma was well liked in the town?"

"Yes, certainly. She was a sweet thing. Thoughtful, but knew her mind. Not that different from you, in fact. A lot of boys in town fancied her but were dissuaded because her family was barely half a step from poverty. She had plenty of friends, though. Have you met dear Polly Kennard yet? She was Emma's chief confidant and one of the few invited to the secret wedding."

Keira nearly blurted *What? The bank robber?* but caught herself in time. Instead, she said, "The florist? She gave me a bunch of flowers yesterday. She seems lovely."

"Oh, she is. She was Emma's closest friend growing up. The murder disturbed Polly greatly. Shortly after it, Polly and her sister, Myrtle, left for one of the big cities and didn't return for close to a decade."

Disturbing her enough to crack her trust in the system and facilitate a slide into a life of crime? Keira shook herself mentally. *Stop getting carried away. Stick to the facts.* "We saw Dane Crispin while we were passing his house. Do you know him well?"

"Hardly at all. He keeps to himself." Adage frowned. "Really, if you're not a fan of the pie, please tell me. I have plenty of other food I can offer you. How about a nice, succulent TV dinner?"

Keira laughed and quickly pushed a forkful of food into her mouth. "Sorry. I got carried away. It really is tasty."

From there, the conversation shifted to present-day events. Adage talked about the sermon he was preparing for the following Sunday, about the fundraiser to repair the church's leaky roof, and how Mrs. Trilby had asked him to spray holy water on her roses because she wanted them to grow faster.

When Keira had finished as much of her plate as would fit inside her, Adage pushed his chair back and folded his hands over his stomach. Blue eyes twinkling behind his glasses, he watched Keira. "Now, there was one other reason I invited you here tonight beyond the enjoyment of your company. I have an offer for you."

"Oh yes?" Keira sat up a little straighter.

"One of my parishioner's sisters in Glendale is looking for a live-in assistant for her bed-and-breakfast. It's a busy little establishment, apparently, and she's seeking someone who will work there in exchange for a room, food, and a modest wage. If you accept, she would like you to start on Friday, in two days' time."

"Oh." *That's so soon.* Keira had to fight to keep any trace of disappointment off her face. "How far away is Glendale?"

"About six hours. I can arrange a lift to a train station in the next town, which will take you the rest of the way." He was watching her closely. "How do you feel about it? I thought it might suit you. Miss Wright is willing to give you all of the training you need, and you'll get cash in hand if you're not able to open a bank account. Plus, my hope is that putting a little distance between you and this town will make it harder for those men to find you. It will be busy work, but I think you're up to the challenge."

"Yes! It sounds perfect. Thank you so much." She made herself smile. *You're not in a position to be picky. This is your opportunity to restart your life. Be grateful.*

Adage nodded. "I'll send word and see about booking that train ticket. Truth be told, I'll be sad to see you go, but I think you'll get along with Miss Wright exceptionally well. It's probably the best outcome I could have hoped for."

"It really is. Let me help with the tidying up."

As Keira dried the dishes and Adage washed, she stared through the kitchen window and watched the mist slide among the forest's trunks. *If I leave on Friday, that gives me tonight, all of tomorrow, and a couple of hours on Friday morning to do everything. To say goodbye to Mason and Zoe. Thank Polly Kennard for the flowers. Thank Adage for the exceptional kindness he's shown. And help a lost spirit...*

"Keira?" Steam from the sink had fogged up Adage's glasses, so he slipped them down his nose to see her better. "Is everything all right?"

Smile, you idiot. "Yes, I'm good! Just a bit tired. It's been a long day." *Tired. Miserable at the thought of leaving Blighty. Frightened of walking through that fog to reach the cottage. Worried that two days won't be enough time to help a woman who has no one else to turn to.*

If my old life was this messy, it's no wonder my brain refuses to remember it.

CHAPTER 18

KEIRA STOOD ON THE edge of the graveyard. Long rectangles of light stretched from the parsonage's windows to paint wan color over the nearest stones. She exhaled, and condensation rose from her lips.

It's not far. Just start walking. You'll be home before you know it.

Her dinner with Adage had gone late. The moon presided high in the sky, surrounded by a crowd of attendant stars. Adage had given her a flashlight to light her way back to the cottage, but despite the lingering clouds, the natural light was strong enough to show her path.

One foot in front of the other. Head down. Senses high. Emma's grave is on the other side of the cottage; you're not going anywhere near her.

Keira tried to keep her eyes fixed on the ground, but it was hard not to look up and play guessing games with the swirling fog, heavy shadows, and cowled stone figures. Shapes seemed to move when she took her eyes off them. She hunted for the prickles along her spine that announced the presence of spirits and sensed a dull touch. It was like having a feather drawn down her back. *They're here, but they're not trying to be felt.*

She paused at the stone fence. The cottage was only a half dozen paces ahead of her, but it felt wrong to keep walking. With so little time left, she couldn't afford to ignore the spirits at her doorstep.

Keira took deliberately slow and even breaths as she turned to face the cemetery. An owl piped its morose call from the woods behind her. A gentle wind ruffled the trees, scratching their branches together to build a discordant, crackling symphony. She felt for the muscle she'd used to see the ghosts the day before. It wasn't easy to find, and for a moment, she thought the ability might have disappeared. Then she felt a twinge of soreness left from straining it and pulled on it to open her eyes.

The mist had thickened in some areas. The effect was barely perceptible, but pools of deeper white clung to certain places even as the fog shifted around them. Keira pushed the ability harder. It sent a sharp, stabbing pain through her skull, but the figures flared into view.

Immediately ahead and twelve grave markers deep, a tall, bone-thin woman watched Keira out of the corner of her eye. She was elderly and dressed in a heavy Victorian gown, complete with bustle, gloves, and hat. As soon as Keira looked at her, she turned and began walking toward the opposite fence, seemingly affronted that Keira would attempt to make eye contact.

Beyond her was an old man, bent nearly double from rheumatism, his only clothing a pair of boxer shorts. He was fainter than the Victorian woman but stood leaning on his gravestone with one hand. Even farther behind him was a small shape still not quite visible. *A child?* Keira strained the muscle more, but the pain shot deep into her head and made her press her palms against her temples. When she opened her eyes again, the figures had vanished.

She took another long, calming breath as she waited for the throbbing headache to dull. Then she wet her lips and took a risk. "Emma, are you here?"

The woman hadn't been visible when Keira had used her second sight, and she didn't appear now, even though Keira knew Emma had the ability to.

She might be ashamed by what she did last night. She could still be angry that I haven't helped. She could have overheard Adage's offer and become disheartened. I wish she'd come out and talk with me again. Maybe making herself visible exhausts her in the same way that using the second sight hurts me?

"Emma, I haven't forgotten my promise. I'm going to help you if I can." Keira balled her hands into fists, trying not to feel too foolish as she talked to the empty cemetery. "Honestly, you haven't given me much to go off, but I'm still going to try. Frank hung himself in the mill. Is he still there? Is he the reason you haven't left this earth?"

No response. Keira dared to pull at the muscle behind her eyes. It was hot agony, but gave her a brief glimpse of the indistinct shapes dotting the graveyard. Emma still wasn't present.

"I'm going to go there. I…I don't have much time left in Blighty and probably won't ever be coming back. But so help me, I'll give this everything I have." No answer. "Well…okay. Good talk."

She turned back to the cottage. As she walked to the door, it was hard not to feel dozens of eyes following her back. *So many spirits. Some that I can't even see clearly. They must all have a reason to linger; I wish I had the time to help them.* The door opened with a groan, and Keira stepped inside, feeling as though her heart were breaking.

Something small and warm rubbed across her leg, and it eased some of her pain. Keira smiled as she bent to pick up the cat. "Hey, Daisy, did you miss me?"

The cat, nearly invisible in the cottage's dark, purred heartily and tried to lick Keira's chin. Keira chuckled as she took her pet back to the fireplace, then cleared away the empty dinner plate, and set about rebuilding the flames.

"Adage found a place for me to stay," she said. The cat stood, tail twitching, watching the flames, then lay down in the same headfirst free fall she'd used when Keira had first found her. She seemed thoroughly unconcerned with Keira's situation. "I'll be leaving the day after tomorrow. Which means I'll need to find you a new home."

She sat on the rug and pulled her knees up under her chin. The fire was growing quickly, but it did little to warm her. "The lady at the bed-and-breakfast probably doesn't want any pets. And…" Her throat hurt, so she swallowed the pain. "And it's probably best for you to stay in Blighty anyway, in case your real owner is eventually found."

Keira glanced at the cat to see her response. Daisy was borderline asleep, and one eye slowly drifted in the wrong direction. Keira didn't know whether to sigh or laugh, so the two mixed together into a weird, mangled cough. She scratched behind the cat's ears and earned fresh purrs for her efforts.

"I'm starting to think you're not magical after all. I've just been talking to a normal stray this whole time, haven't I?"

The cat lifted her head to look at Keira, her lips parted, and for a fraction of a second, Keira actually expected Daisy to speak. Then she burped, rolled over, and closed her eyes.

Keira threw her head back and laughed. The chuckles shook her, refusing to abate until tears pricked at her eyes. She wiped them away as she finally managed to regain her breath and stretched her legs out to warm them. "Okay, I think that's enough with the pity party. I've got work to do."

The clock above the mantel said it was nearly ten. Keira didn't trust Blighty's streets to be completely deserted, so she rose and began gathering equipment as she waited.

There wasn't much to put together. She set the flashlight and a small kitchen knife on the round table, then pulled on extra layers of sweaters and pants. After swapping Adage's donated sneakers for her thicker boots, she paced.

The clock seemed to move agonizingly slowly, and Keira, trapped with her thoughts, felt half an inch from insanity by the time it chimed eleven. She'd intended to wait for midnight for caution's sake but figured eleven was close enough.

"Don't wait up, Daisy." Keira tucked the flashlight and the

knife into her jeans' pockets. The night was bright enough that she wouldn't need the flashlight until she reached her destination, and she hoped the knife wouldn't be necessary at all. She crept out of the cottage, put her chilled hands into her pockets, and hurried through the mist.

The tendrils clung to her like hundreds of disembodied fingers. She kept her eyes focused ahead until she'd passed through the bushy divider that separated her cemetery from the normal world. Just like she'd noticed the day before, the air was a degree or two warmer away from the tombstones.

Adage's windows were dark, but Keira still took care to keep her footfalls quiet as she slunk past. She picked her pace up again once she reached the lane and hurried toward the main street.

As she'd hoped, the town was silent. A few buildings still had lights on, but there were no cars or pedestrians on the road. Keira pulled her hoodie up to hide her face just in case. What she had planned wasn't strictly illegal, but it would probably be frowned upon and prompt a series of questions that wouldn't be easy to answer.

She jogged through the town's residential section and into the rural areas. The street was almost unrecognizable under the moon's cold light. Keira had begun to question whether she was going in the right direction, until the wall of ivy to her left identified the Crispin estate. She was tempted to slow and peek through the gate once again, but instead fixed her eyes ahead and quickened her pace.

Before long, the mill loomed into view. Keira slowed to a brisk walk. Her breathing was rough, and she was looking forward to washing the sweat off once she returned to the cottage, but the run had done its job of warming her core. She paused on the edge of the field, then took a deep breath and stepped into the long, weedy grass.

Now that she was expecting it, she registered the change instantly. The temperature began to plummet as tiny chills crawled up her limbs.

It felt different that night, though. During her first encounter with the mill, she hadn't realized what was happening until she was standing in the thick of it. This time, she was prepared for the sensation of suffering. She let it wash over her, felt its thousand facets, and tasted its intensity. The emotional imprint was strong enough to sway her for a moment, but then she swallowed, pushed the sensation down, waited until her head was clear, and kept walking.

She pulled the flashlight out of her pocket as she moved toward the window Zoe had looked through earlier that day. The glass was blurred with grime and shrouded in cobwebs, but she leaned close, turned on the flashlight, and aimed it inside.

A jumble of shapes emerged under her light. Great machines, long dormant, dominated the room, and a medley of abandoned furniture was scattered around it. It was hard to see clearly through the glass, so she stepped back and looked for a way in. The huge doors stood farther down the building. Keira could visualize the workers filing through every morning and the metal doors slamming shut behind them. Shivers dug their way down her spine.

As she neared the doors, she saw their handles had been chained together. She rattled the binds, but they didn't come loose. The metal looked ancient—it had probably been installed when the mill closed—but like the brick building, it hadn't yet deteriorated enough to break.

Zoe and Mason said kids went into the mill. There must be a way inside.

Keira began circling the building and shone her flashlight over every part of the wall she passed. Most of the windows were broken, but none were large enough or low enough for her to worm her way through.

At last, at the back of the building, she found a window that had come out of its frame completely. A stack of decayed crates and barrels were packed underneath to act as crude stairs.

She wasn't sure she could trust the rotting wood to take her weight, but it seemed the only option. Keira put the flashlight's handle between her teeth and carefully lifted herself onto the first crate. It groaned but didn't collapse. She kept her breathing shallow as she shuffled onto the highest barrel, then eased toward the window. The opening was barely large enough for her to fit, but she managed by squeezing her shoulder blades together and wiggling her torso through. She hung there as she spat the flashlight back into her hand and shone it on the ground below.

The kids had stacked piles of wool below the window to cushion their landing. Even from her perch ten feet above, she could smell a disgusting musk that was the result of centuries of exposure to the elements. She held her breath as she dropped onto it.

The bundle of wool exhaled a series of sharp cries as she landed, and dozens of tiny shapes flicked away from her light. She'd accidentally disturbed a mouse nest. *Mason might have come here as a child, but I doubt any of the most recent generation have stepped into the building. I don't blame them. If I had the choice between this and TV, I know which I'd pick.*

Keira straightened and turned her flashlight across the mill. It was an open room—probably bitterly cold during winter and boiling hot in summer—with a row of offices along one wall.

The machines took up nearly half of the building, and the other half was filled with long, low tables where the workers could sort through the wool. The shadows they cast fluttered along the brick walls and across the ceiling. Keira exhaled, and the plume of telltale mist drifted away from her.

"Frank?" She hated that her voice was shaking, but so were her legs. "Frank Crispin? My name is Keira. I'm here to help you."

CHAPTER 19

AS THE ECHOES OF Keira's voice faded, she lowered her guard and allowed the mill's emotions to flood around her. Generations of suffering, fear, and pain hit her like a punch and dropped her to her knees. Keira retched, doubling over, but her body wasn't trying to expel food. It was trying to purge itself of the echoes of past lives.

She knew the sensation would stop if she tried to block it, but instead, she opened herself to it, welcoming every hateful, hurtful memory the spirits wanted to give her. To her surprise, the pain had an end. She started to taste different emotions. There was hope—the poor worker woman whose wealthy aunt had invited her to visit. Joy—a healthy child had been born. Love. Laughter. Kindness. Generosity.

Keira touched her face. Her cheeks were wet with tears she didn't remember shedding. The flood of memories, both the pleasant and the painful, swelled inside her, threatening to overwhelm her, then abated, like a receding wave.

Keira sucked in a breath. Dizziness made her want to curl into a ball and wait for the sensations to pass, but she had a task to complete. She found the aching muscle and pulled on it to open her second sight.

The mill was full of the translucent spirits. Some had striking features and black eyes; others appeared as dull blurs. Many watched her, but others paced restlessly or sat at the tables. She saw old-fashioned construction uniforms; those were the workers who had perished while building the mill. She saw a large man with his shirt unbuttoned and a sweaty face; death from a heart attack, she thought. Several women, sickly looking, clustered together in the same way they must have taken solace from each other in life.

And then there were the accidental deaths. Limbs torn off by the whirring machine rotors. Faces blistered from boiling water. One woman had blood dribbling from her eyes, cheek, and lips, where she had been beaten to death.

Keira counted more than thirty spirits, and their clothing styles spanned at least fifty years. She took another breath to clear her head. "Which of you is Frank Crispin?"

None of the spirits moved for a moment, then the sweaty man with the unbuttoned shirt approached. He was too old to be Frank—he looked at least fifty—but his clothes suggested he ranked above the menial workers surrounding him. A foreman, Keira thought, or perhaps one of the accountants. His smile was unexpectedly kind as he beckoned to her.

The muscle screamed from the prolonged use, and Keira struggled to keep it active as she rose and stumbled after the foreman. He led her to a clear section of the floor, then glanced upward. One finger pointed toward the ceiling, then lowered as though drawing an invisible line and traced around his throat.

Keira looked up. A metal pipe ran above their heads, four feet out of reach. "Is this where Frank hung himself?"

The foreman nodded, the sweat dotting his face glistening in her flashlight's beam.

"But his spirit didn't linger?"

He spread his hands and shook his head.

Damn.

She turned to look across the mill. Its spirits, so faint they were nearly invisible in the low light, had gathered around, watching her with dead eyes. Seeing them trapped there, waiting for something or someone that would likely never come, was agonizing.

"I'm sorry," she said, but she found it difficult to verbalize what she was sorry for. *Everything, I suppose. I'm sorry that you died here. I'm sorry that you couldn't move on. I'm sorry I can't help.*

Unbearable pain radiated through her head. She relaxed the muscle, and the figures faded from sight. The relief nearly dropped Keira to her knees again, and she grabbed the back of a nearby chair to stabilize herself.

Prickles sparked where her skin touched the wood. They coursed up her arm, stinging like a low electrical current. She blinked, and suddenly, her eyes showed her a new sight.

She was still in the mill, but it was no longer night. A bloodred sunset sent violent stripes of color through the narrow windows and painted them across the floor. A thin, dark-haired man walked through the room. His black suit was disheveled, and his face blotchy and wet with tears. A length of rope hung from one hand, dragging over the floor and creating paths through the dust. Keira blinked again and saw the man throwing the rope over the pipe. Then he was tying one end into a noose. Climbing onto the chair Keira had rested against. Tightening the rope. Kicking the chair away.

A choked cry escaped Keira as she watched Frank Crispin spasm on the end of his rope. Then she blinked and was back in the present, shaking and exhausted, one hand pressed over her mouth to silence the cries. Her legs collapsed and sent her tumbling to the ground.

Icy chills ran along her arms and her back, and she had a horrible idea that the mill's spirits had clustered forward to touch her. She tried to pull on the ability that allowed her to see them, but it did nothing except stab pain across her skull. She'd overused the muscle.

Keira put her hands on her knees and focused on breathing deeply. Bit by bit, she began to block out the emotions, gradually reducing her exposure to the mill's effect until her head had cleared enough to think.

Frank Crispin isn't here. If Emma is waiting for him, he's already moved on.

She raised her head. The mill, mottled by shadows, appeared

desolate in her flashlight's beam, but she couldn't forget the thin, baleful faces that had watched her. She wanted to say something, but words failed her. Comfort would be hollow. Promises couldn't be met. Sympathy would feel trite. All she could manage was to echo herself. "I'm sorry."

Chills grazed her cheek, brushing at the tears there. She shivered as the liquid turned to frost. The invisible fingers lingered for a moment, then retreated.

Slowly, feeling as though she'd stepped in front of a freight train, Keira regained her feet. She stumbled to the pile of wool below the window. The sill was high, but she rested her forearms on it and scrambled up. As she slid through the opening, she managed to twist her body and hold on to the ledge while lowering her legs toward the external wood pallet steps. She ended up with her body outside and her head poised in the window. Keira directed the flashlight into the mill a final time, looking over the last resting place for dozens of souls and said a word that made her stomach shrivel in misery: "Goodbye."

The walk back to the parsonage was a slow, bitter one. She'd seen Frank's death, but no help had come from it. He'd moved on—probably at the same moment as he'd died—and her instincts told her that bit of information wouldn't be news to Emma.

On top of that, the cluster of souls waiting inside the mill set her heart aching. They had already been there for decades. Who knew how much longer they would linger in the loveless, lifeless shell of the building? Would they be stuck there until the Earth dissolved and life was extinguished? She exhaled and pushed her hands into her pockets. She hated herself for not being able to help. But with one day left in Blighty, she was no closer to saving the first spirit she'd promised assistance to.

The thoughts consumed Keira so completely that she forgot to feel anxious as she walked through the cemetery's mist. She paused at the gate leading to her cottage and turned back to the gravestones. Her headache was still strong enough that she knew attempting to invoke her second sight would be stupid, so she spoke to an invisible audience. "Emma? I went to the mill. Frank died in it. But he's no longer there. He moved on."

The graveyard was still. Keira waited, watching the mist, and finally shrugged. "I guess you already knew that. I'm sorry, Emma."

Inside, the cottage was blissfully warm, and Keira shed her extra clothing. The bed was tempting, but a layer of dried sweat forced her into the shower. Even though she washed quickly, by the time she'd braided her wet hair, it was nearly two in the morning.

She belly flopped into the bed and groaned happily at how soft it felt. A small, warm shape jumped up beside her and began kneading at her back. "G'night, Daisy," Keira mumbled, and she was asleep even before the cat had finished licking her face.

CHAPTER 20

SPEARS OF LIGHT CUT across Keira's face. She squinted and rolled onto her other side, dislodging the warm cat from her shoulder. Daisy stretched, yawned, and flopped onto her other side.

"Morning," Keira mumbled as the cat started purring. "Thanks for sticking with me last night. I'm not normally such a miserable wet blanket, I promise."

The cat rubbed its head against Keira's back, and she chuckled as she reached over to scratch Daisy's chin. "You're hungry, huh? Gimme a minute."

As she rolled out of bed, she checked the clock on the fireplace mantel. It was nearly ten. Keira groaned and scrambled into some clothes. *That's so not fair. I swear I was asleep for no more than five minutes.*

She hopped into the kitchen, put the kettle on, and set about giving Daisy her breakfast. As she watched the cat eat, some of the sadness from the previous evening threatened to suck her back in. It was a bright, crisp morning, and the sun that flooded through the windows gave the cottage a welcoming glow. The weather, the comfortable surroundings, and the little cat all reminded Keira of how much she was about to lose.

Suck it up. Keira braced her shoulders, turned, and plucked a clean cup off the draining board. She added a tea bag and flexed her neck as she waited on the kettle. *Your problems are obnoxiously trivial, everything considered. You've gone and attached yourself to this area, probably because you don't remember anything before it. But Glendale could be equally nice. You might even make friends there. And I'd hazard to guess, it probably has its fair share of ghosts for you to worry over.*

Despite trying to make light of the situation, Keira felt a fresh cut of grief as she remembered the trapped souls she was leaving behind. She inhaled deeply, plucked the kettle off its stand, and filled her mug. The rest of the water went toward cooking a bowl of rice. She leaned against the kitchen counter while the water boiled, her legs crossed and the cup clasped in her hands to ward off the early morning chills. She watched as Daisy finished her meal and went about exploring the cottage.

I have one day left in this town. I should spend it wisely. If only Emma would talk to me, I'd know where to look, instead of running all over the countryside like this. She asked for help, which means her problem must have an answer I can find, but what else is there to explore?

Keira only had one remaining theory: George Crispin hadn't been the killer. It seemed increasingly unlikely after Adage's testimony, but without any stronger lead, she had to follow it.

"That's the problem, though. What sort of evidence could survive forty years without the police finding it?" she asked Daisy, who was eyeing the wardrobe beside the bed.

The cat crouched, wiggled her hind quarters, and leaped for the narrow ledge on top of the cupboard. She made it—barely— and Keira raised a cheer.

The rice seemed close enough to being cooked, so Keira drained the excess water and ate it out of the saucepan. She ran over the conundrum in her mind as she chewed. The answer came to her after a moment, and it was so obvious that she could have smacked herself for not figuring it out earlier.

For evidence to survive this long, it can't be physical. It can't be something that will decay or be washed away or break. It has to be something like...memories.

Adage had said Emma's closest friend was Polly Kennard. The florist had been so distressed by her companion's death that she'd left the town for close to a decade. If anyone in Blighty was going to have the key to unmasking Emma's killer, it would be Polly.

Keira scarfed down the remainder of her breakfast, washed the pot at breakneck speed, and pulled on a sweater before racing toward the door. A heavy thud told her the little cat had come down from her perch, and Keira let her outside. "Don't stray too far, okay?"

The cat frisked into the cemetery and began nosing about the gravestones. Keira could only hope none of the spirits would be offended and began jogging to town.

The narrow dirt road was becoming increasingly familiar. She recognized the oddly shaped shrubs, the potholes, and the row of tall trees that housed countless birds. Melancholy threatened again, but she shoved it into the back of her conscience.

The town was alive by the time she reached it. Jangling doorbells echoed around her, and raucous laughter came from near the fountain. Keira entered the florist's and found Polly Kennard at the counter, ringing up a huge bunch of roses for an older gentleman. Keira turned toward the flower-lined walls and pretended to admire the bouquets while Polly finished the sale.

At last, the door jingled, signaling that the other shopper had left, and Keira turned. To her shock, Polly was already standing next to her, beaming eagerly behind her pince-nez glasses. "After more flowers, dear?"

Keira laughed and pressed a hand to her heart. "Thank you, but I'd better not take any more of your stock. I just came in to thank you for yesterday's beautiful daisies."

"Anytime, my dear, anytime." Polly seized Keira's arm and pulled her toward the back of the store. "You still haven't met my son, have you? You're in luck—he's home today. Normally, Harry's out practicing with his friends. He's in a band, you see. Do you like musicians? Of course you do. Young ladies love musicians. He's the lead singer, you know." Then she called up the recessed stairs hidden behind the counter, "Harry, it's that lovely lady I was telling you about yesterday! Come on down and meet Miss Keira!"

Keira, unable to get a word in edgewise, could only grimace as heavy footsteps moved down the stairs. In her excitement to make progress on Emma's mystery, she'd completely forgotten that Polly had been trying to play matchmaker for her son. "Uh, actually—"

Polly didn't give her a chance to object but patted her arm conspiratorially. "I'm sure you two will get on like a house on fire. He's such a sweet boy."

The footsteps came to a halt, and Harry emerged from the shadows. Keira felt her eyebrows rise, and despite knowing how rude she was being, she was incapable of stopping herself from staring.

Blighty was a charming, respectable, pretty sort of town. Its houses were quaint, its countryside was green and soothing, and its stores were cozy and welcoming. Harry Kennard looked more out of place than a crow in a whitest-dove contest.

His shoulder-length, uncomfortably straight hair had been dyed black. His eyes and lips were painted. Even his piercings were made of black plastic. It was hard to tell if he was naturally pale or if he used powder to achieve his ideal shade of pallid, but the effect was certainly striking. He was tall enough that his head brushed the doorway's top, even though he stooped, and he gave Keira a dispassionate blink with two flat, resigned eyes.

Keira tried to push through the shock and fix a polite smile onto her face as she glanced between the sweet, motherly Polly and her son. "Wow. Uh. Hey. Nice to meet you."

He gave Keira one very long, very unimpressed stare before turning on the spot and retreating up the stairs.

"Good thought, Harry, let's have a cup of tea," Polly tittered. She squeezed Keira's arm and leaned close. "He likes you."

She thought her face might break from the fake smile. "Yay."

Before Keira knew what was happening, Polly had whisked to the store's front entrance and flipped the flowery *Open* placard so that the rainy-weather *Closed* side faced outside. As the florist locked the door, Keira had just enough time to wish she were anywhere else in the world, literally anywhere—then Polly was dragging her up the stairs to the apartment above the shop.

Well, I still need to talk to her. Even if she's trying to set me up with her son, this might be my best opportunity.

Upstairs was a cozy, cluttered apartment. Very little of Harry existed in the space; the upholstery and wallpapers were in floral prints that featured shades of pinks, oranges, yellows, and greens. Cherubic figurines cluttered every surface. Only one ornament seemed to have been chosen by the man: a bleached-white skull perched on top of the entertainment unit. Keira squinted at it. The skull was crumbly and asymmetrical enough for her to think it might be real.

"Harry!" Polly fussed around the space, directing Keira to a rose-patterned couch, then bustling into the kitchen. "Harry, don't slink off into your room when we have guests! It's not polite!"

Keira could hear a long, exaggerated sigh from the end of the hallway. She leaned forward to glimpse Harry reemerge from his room, which was painted entirely in shades of black, from what she could see. He slouched back into the living room.

"Oh good, there you are. I bet you wanted to brush your hair. Cheeky boy." Polly pushed her son into the seat opposite Keira and began setting out a fine china tea set.

For a moment, Keira and Harry were in danger of sharing some exceptionally awkward eye contact, but Harry spared her from it by flopping back and staring at the ceiling.

Keira was surprised by a sudden rush of sympathy for Polly. The florist was giving everything she had to make a good first impression for her son; the china was clearly only for special occasions, and her nervous chattering served to underline how eager she was. But her chances of success were less than zero. Even if Keira had been interested in the brooding goth, he was clearly not interested in her. Or, she suspected, in much of anything.

"Let me help you with that," Keira said, hoping she could subvert the awkwardness by spending the visit with her host. But Polly shooed her back to the couch. "Don't be silly, honey. I've got this sorted. I'm sure you two want to get to know each other."

Keira had no choice but to slide back into her seat. Harry continued to ignore her in favor of watching the white paint above his head. She cleared her throat and tried to find some way to break the silence. Her eyes landed on his hands, which he'd rested in his lap. "Nice nails."

His head straightened, and he gave another incredibly long, incredibly slow blink. "They're black."

Keira could only manage a tight-lipped nod. "They definitely are."

Polly appeared at their side, a tray of cups balanced in her hands. "Here we go, kids. How do you like yours, Keira? Tea? Coffee? Or I could make some hot chocolate if you—"

"Tea's fine," Keira quickly interjected. "Uh, milk, no sugar, thanks."

"Absolutely, dear. Harry, why don't you invite Keira to your next band rehearsal? You have such a pretty voice. I'm sure she'd enjoy it."

Another heavy, laborious sigh escaped Harry. "It's post-transient death grunge. You're not supposed to enjoy it."

"Harry," his mother hissed, kicking at his foot. He ignored her.

Keira tried her best to divert the conversation. "You have a gorgeous store. I admire it every time I pass by."

"Ooh, thank you, dear!" Polly almost glowed. "It's my pride and joy. My sister owns the coffeehouse by the fountain. Has Beans and Two Bees. Clever, eh?"

Harry's lips pulled back from his teeth in a grimace at the same time as Keira said, "Yes, very."

"And you're visiting with nice Mr. Adage, aren't you, Keira?"

"Yes. He's been very kind to let me stay." Keira glanced at Harry, who was pointedly ignoring them. She knew she shouldn't prod him, but the opportunity was too good to pass up. "Harry, I bet you can appreciate a good cemetery."

His ocher-lined eyes lit on her. "I do. I visit it at night and sit beneath the stones and imagine I'm sinking down, down, down, into my tomb."

"*Harry!*" Polly sounded scandalized. She tweaked her son's ear, shaking his long hair into disarray. Keira tensed up, expecting a fight, but Harry simply ran his fingers through his locks and leaned back in the chair. A potato would have shown more emotion.

Deep mortification flushed color over Polly's cheeks and widened her eyes. "I'm sure he's just joking, dear. He's really quite a sweet boy. He writes his own songs, you know; he's very good at it."

"They're all about pain and death."

"*Harry.*"

"Oh good, my favorite." Keira was trying furiously not to laugh. She knew her face muscles were twitching and could only hope that Polly was so distracted by her son that she didn't notice.

Polly's smile was very near cracking. She sat on the edge of her seat, shooting desperate glances between Keira and Harry, with her hands clasped in her lap. "He plays in the local pub sometimes. You should come along for one of his concerts."

Harry added, "I like to see how quickly we can empty the place. My record is six minutes."

Polly loosed another strained, desperate laugh. "You're such a joker, Harry. People love your little songs. And…and…" She was clearly clutching at straws but refused to give up. "He's quite artistic too! If painting everything you own black counts—"

"Mum." Harry's voice carried no inflection. "You have a store to watch."

She gave a small, defeated exhale and rose. "Yes, yes, of course. I'll leave you two to get to know each other better. No rush, Keira, no rush at all! There's plenty more tea!"

They both waited as Polly hurried to the stairs, shot them a hopeful glance over her shoulder, and descended out of sight.

Silence filled the room. Keira let her eyes rove over the decorations. Unable to tolerate the silence, she cleared her throat. "So—"

Harry, still staring blandly at the opposite wall, raised a finger to indicate he wanted silence. After a moment, Keira understood why: a door clicked, betraying that Polly had given up eavesdropping at the base of the stairs.

Harry let his head loll to one side, his limp, dark hair half covering his eyes. "You live in the graveyard?"

"Well, right on the edge of it, if that counts."

Apparently it did, because Harry gave her one slow nod. "Cool."

Keira cleared her throat. "Sorry about this by the way."

"Not the first time. Won't be the last." He sighed in a way that suggested he'd accepted his fate. "I think she's running out of people inside the town. She's starting to outsource."

He continued to watch the opposite wall, and the lack of eye contact was beginning to unnerve Keira. She drained her cup of tea, scorching her tongue in the process.

Finally, the corners of his lips twitched. It wasn't much—the memory of a smile if that—but Keira thought it was more than most people saw. "You'd better go before Mum invents an excuse to trap you here longer."

"I'll do that. But first, can I ask you something?"

His eyebrows rose.

"Is that a real skull?"

Harry followed her gaze toward the white shape on top of the entertainment unit. "Mum thinks it's plastic."

"But…it's not?"

His unblinking stare held a deep, secret humor. "Goodbye, Keira."

She bit the inside of her mouth so that she wouldn't be tempted to laugh, returned her cup to the table, and rose. "Sure thing. Maybe I'll see you around the graveyard sometime."

Keira could feel his eyes on her back as she hurried down the stairs and back into the florist shop. *He's weird as heck, but he doesn't seem bad. I get the feeling he's actually quite smart under his eighteen layers of makeup.*

Polly was at the counter, furiously snipping ribbons, and looked up as Keira entered. Tentative hope flitted across her face. "He, uh, he wasn't on his best form today, but he's normally quite the charmer."

Lying to Polly would have been abhorrent, but Keira didn't want to entirely crush her either. Instead, she chose to employ something close to the truth. "He seems like a cool guy. I wouldn't mind getting to know him more—as friends."

"Yes?" Polly looked ready to hug Keira, who quickly sidled around the desk to put some distance between them.

"As friends," she repeated, but Polly seemed deaf to the phrase. She looked ready to burst out of her skin. *There's no time like the present*, Keira thought helplessly, and launched into her question before her host could sing any more of her son's praises. "Polly, I've been learning as much as I can about this town, and Emma Carthage's story keeps coming up. You knew her, didn't you?"

For the first time since Keira had entered the store, Polly's flawless smile dropped. She blinked, looking stunned, as though Keira had slapped her. Then she chuckled weakly, turned to the cut ribbons, and began to roll them absentmindedly. "Oh, yes, yes, we used to be friends back in the day."

Polly clearly disliked the subject, and Keira very nearly backed out. The emotional scab had to be raw, still—but Polly's memories might be Emma's last chance to move on. "I was hoping to learn more about her death. Especially about her killer."

Polly shoved the ribbon spools onto their shelf too quickly, and two rolls tumbled back off and bounced over the wooden floor. Her fingers were shaking as she picked them up. "He was… He…" Her face contorted, then the sweet, grandmotherly smile was back in place like an unbreakable mask. "You're really testing my memory, dear. You'd much better ask some other people about it. Adage knows most of the business."

Her chance was slipping away, and Keira desperately tried to snatch it back. "You remember Frank, though, don't you? Emma's fiancé?"

Polly glanced aside and hesitated. For a second, Keira worried she'd be stonewalled again, but then the florist spoke. "Yes. Of course. Frank… People say he was weak willed, but he would have done anything for Emma. They would have been happy.

Bought a little house in the country, maybe. Raised a family. He should have known…"

Keira leaned over the countertop hopefully. "Yes?"

"Oh, never mind my rambling, dear. I was just remembering… You know how sometimes you have the opportunity to do the right thing, and you want to, and you're preparing to, but then the chance evaporates, and all you can do is spend the rest of your life regretting that you waited too long?"

Lady, I have less than four days stored in my memory banks. That is not a situation I've encountered in that time. "Sure?"

Polly sighed heavily. "Then you'll understand me when I say this: if life gives you a chance for something, you can't hesitate or wait for a better time. You just have to take a leap of faith while it's there."

Keira was nodding, but her brain was composed entirely of question marks. "Do you regret something that happened before Emma's death?"

A flash of panic crossed the florist's face. She glanced behind herself, then busied her hands with stripping leaves off a bunch of flowers in a bucket behind her desk. "She came to my house on the morning she died. I wasn't home; my sister answered the door, but dear Emma wouldn't come in. She left for Crispin House without waiting for me to come back. Sometimes I think…if I'd been there for her…if I'd guessed…" Polly shook her head, reached over the counter, and seized Keira's hands. She tilted forward so she could give a meaningful look over the pince-nez glasses. "Regret is a terrible thing, my dear. I hope I'm not being too blunt—but if there's a special someone you think you might have feelings for…"

Oh. We're back to that. Keira very carefully extracted her hands. "I understand. Thank you, Polly. You've been incredibly kind today."

The smile was back in place. "Anytime, dear, anytime. Pop back in if you fancy some flowers; anything in the shop is yours!"

Nodding and muttering thanks, Keira backed out of the store—and collided with a tall, warm body. "Ah, I'm so sorry." She turned and blinked up at a familiar smile.

"You weren't having tea with Harry, were you?" Mason tilted his head to one side, his warm green eyes sparkling with laughter. "You'll make me jealous."

CHAPTER 21

KEIRA LAUGHED AND GAVE Mason's shoulder a shove as she slipped past him. "Harry sure is something, isn't he? Does he really have concerts at the pub?"

"Oh, yes. They're incredible." Mason nodded in the direction of the town center, and they began strolling toward the fountain. "Ear-splitting screams count as incredible, right?"

"Ha!" Keira pushed her hands into her pockets and matched Mason's easy pace. "What're you doing out this way?"

"On my way to visit you, in actual fact. It's lucky I saw you as I was passing the florist." He shrugged. "My official excuse was to check on your arm, but really, I was just bored. Can I buy you a drink?"

You need to tell him you're leaving. Keira's chest tightened at the thought, but she smiled before the emotion could leak onto her face. "Can we get it to-go? Today's too nice to sit inside."

"Good thought; we should enjoy the sun while it lasts. They're talking about more rain tonight." They'd reached the intersection, and even though there weren't any cars in sight, Mason still stopped and looked both ways before leading Keira across. "That's one of my favorite things about Blighty: it's almost perpetually wet. If it's not rain, it's mist, and if it's not mist, it's snow that turns to slush before you can look sideways at it."

Their conversation came to a halt as they entered the coffee shop and a wave of chatter and radio tunes enveloped them. Keira only remembered her financially handicapped condition when they'd joined the queue. "Uh…sorry, I didn't bring any money—"

"Good! It's my treat."

Marlene, the disengaged barista, barely glanced at them before asking what they wanted. Keira crossed her fingers that she didn't hate coffee and asked for a latte. Mason ordered tea for himself. Keira didn't know how it was possible when Marlene only had one harried-looking assistant helping her, but their orders were filled in less than a minute.

Keira wrapped her hands around her cardboard cup and inhaled deeply as she returned to the outdoors.

Mason nodded toward the fountain. "Want to sit for a minute?"

The stone ledge surrounding the feature was still cold, even though they settled on the sunny side. Keira hadn't been close enough to see the fountain clearly before, and she couldn't help but gawk. It was a bizarre sculpture: cherubic toddlers with fish tails frolicked up Grecian pillars. Every few meters, an openmouthed gargoyle vomited water into the basin below. The spectacle was topped with a crossbow-toting centaur endowed with one of the largest noses she'd ever seen.

"What do you think?" Mason watched her with open amusement.

She shook her head. "It's... Wow. There's something for everyone, huh?"

"It was made by Perrault, a well-known local sculptor. He wasn't acclaimed, mind. Just...well-known."

Keira snickered and turned back to her drink. From her seat, they could see down both main roads and watch the townspeople hurry about their lives. The water gurgled behind them, the relaxing sound blending into the noises emitted from the various stores. Mason sat close, and she could almost feel the happiness radiating from him. He seemed to be in an exceptionally good mood, which made her news all the more difficult to share.

Putting it off will only make it harder. Keira scuffed her feet over the ground as she tried to find a pleasant way to phrase the announcement. *Knock, knock! Who's there? Not me. I'm outta this place!*

"Keira? Everything okay?"

"Sure." She held her smile but couldn't look at him. "Adage found me a job and a place to stay. In Glendale."

Mason didn't reply for a moment. When he spoke, his voice had lost its bright tone. "That's fast."

"It is, isn't it?"

Warm fingers brushed her cheek, then slipped under her chin.

He very gently turned her head until she could no longer avoid looking at him. Worry clouded his face. His eyebrows pulled together, and his angular cheeks appeared even more prominent without the familiar grin softening them. "You look so sad."

Smile, Keira. She fought to keep her voice from cracking. "It's stupid, isn't it? It's not like I've lived in Blighty my whole life or anything. I'm sure Glendale is a great town. I just…"

His mouth twitched, and his eyebrows tugged even closer together. "Tell Adage you want to stay."

She carefully pulled free from his fingers. He let her go, but his thumb grazed her jaw before it withdrew. Keira steeled herself, then said, "I don't want to do that. He's already given me so much. I'd be the world's most entitled jerk to ask for more. Besides, he says Blighty is a closed town when it comes to jobs. No one would hire me, and I can't live for long without an income."

Mason turned aside, seeming agitated. His fingers drummed against the fountain's stone bench as he chewed at the inside of his cheek. "I have a spare room you're welcome to. And I'll help you find a local job. People here like me. They'll hire you if I put in a good word."

Keira chuckled as she patted his arm. "It's okay, Mason. I really, really appreciate it, but you don't have to fix every problem in the world. Besides, you yourself said it would be safer if I had some distance between myself and Blighty, just in case those men are still looking for me. And…maybe it'll be healthy for me to stretch a little. Adage found me a good, honest job. I'll probably like it. Who knows? I might even love it."

He lapsed into silence for several long minutes, though his fingers continued their restless tapping. When Keira glanced at him, his gaze was distant. He seemed to be thinking something through, so she gave him time. Eventually, he inhaled and turned back to her. Though it had lost its carefree ease, his smile was back in place, and his voice was no longer tight. "Glendale's only…what? Six hours away? I'll come and visit sometimes."

"No, you don't have to do that."

"Course I do. I keep telling you I have too much time on my hands." At last, the fingers stopped drumming. He picked up his cup but didn't drink from it. "When are you leaving?"

"Tomorrow morning."

He blew a breath out. "Wow. Okay. I'll come and see you off at the station. Need any help packing?"

This time, when she laughed, it didn't even hurt. "Thanks, but I'll take care of it. Though I'm not sure how I'll fit all two pairs of pants into my travel case."

"Ha, fair enough."

"But there is something you could help me with."

"Yeah?" He tilted his head to one side, and Keira's chest ached at the sight. No matter where she went, she doubted anyone would be able to replicate that motion quite so well.

"I need a home for Daisy. Somewhere that will take good care of her. You still like cats, right?"

"Sure do. Leave her with me; she'll be treated like a queen."

"Thank you. That's a weight off my mind." Keira took a sip

from her cup and discovered she did, in fact, hate coffee. She pulled a face, and Mason's amusement was evident.

"Don't like it?"

"Not in the slightest."

"Here, let's swap." He took her cup out of her hand and replaced it with his own before she could object. He swirled the drink for a moment, his eyes thoughtful, then said, "Can I ask an odd question?"

"Go for it."

"What's your favorite dinosaur?"

"Huh. I don't know." Keira put her head back as she thought. "Guess I'd have to go with the velociraptor. The claws are pretty cool."

"Did you learn about them through a movie or a book?"

"No…not that I remember anyway."

"Hmm." Mason gave her a searching look, and Keira lifted her eyebrows.

"I'm guessing you prefer the T-rex?"

"Ha! No, just…trying to puzzle something out. I don't think your memory loss is a typical case. I wasn't sure whether I should say something, but…well, if you're leaving, you'd better know now."

Keira sat a little straighter. Mason's expression suggested he didn't have good news, so she waited quietly for him to collect his thoughts.

"There are basically two types of learning," he said at last, and he put his cup aside. "Implicit and declarative. Implicit is for things that become subconscious or muscle memory, such as walking or playing the piano or being able to speak. Declarative is more focused on conscious learning, like remembering the queen's name or movie plots or your friends' faces.

"When someone suffers from memory loss, they usually lose the declarative but retain most of the implicit—an artist could forget his wife but still be able to paint. I thought this was what had happened to you. You seem generally healthy and mentally sound; you just can't remember anything. But strangely, you seemed to have retained certain declarative memories as well."

"Ah, like the velociraptors?"

"Exactly." Mason rubbed at the back of his neck. "You remember the dinosaur, but not when or how you learned about it. Correct me if I'm off mark here, but it seems like the only part of your memory that's been damaged is the part that relates to *you*: your experiences, your opinions, your identity."

Keira stared at the ground. She dug through her mind again, searching for stray memories. Knowing what to look for, she realized she actually had retained a swath of knowledge. She'd known what Zoe had meant when she'd referred to James Bond. She could remember that the sun went down in the west. Mason's hair color reminded her of chocolate. But she didn't know what chocolate tasted like. She couldn't remember ever seeing the sun set. She didn't know which James Bond movies she'd watched or whether she'd enjoyed them. It was unnerving, and she put aside her cup so she could wrap her arms around her torso defensively. "What does that mean?"

He shook his head. "I have no idea. I researched it late through last night, but I couldn't find any comparable cases. Generally, patients either lose all of their memories or just a segment of time. I've never heard of a case where an identity is erased but the rest is left untouched. It's bizarre."

Keira scowled at the stone path surrounding the fountain. "Just once, it might be nice to be normal."

"Hey." Mason's knuckle nudged the underside of her chin, bringing her attention back to him. "I'm sorry. I didn't mean to upset you. Like I said the other day, we still don't fully understand how memories are stored. This could be a normal, albeit extremely uncommon, variation." His eyes seemed to darken a fraction. "I just wish I could do more to help. This can't be pleasant for you."

Keira deliberately relaxed her pose. "It's not that bad, actually. I can't miss what I don't remember. And you and Zoe have been amazingly kind; I never expected to feel so welcomed here."

"Zoe's going to miss you like crazy. Most people don't have time for her or her theories, and I know she's started thinking of you as her friend." He scratched at the back of his neck. "I guess all three of us were looking for some kind of friendship."

Keira snorted. "No, I don't believe that about you for a second, Mr. Congeniality. You said it yourself: this town loves you."

"You'd be surprised. I've been feeling lost since I came back from med school. I was gone for nearly four years. Most of my friends have moved away, and the only one who's still here has changed so much that it's hard to recognize him. You're right—people do like me, but in a detached, he's-a-good-kid sort of way. There's no one I can really talk to. Meeting you was like…like…" His gaze became distant for a moment, but then he clapped his hands on his knees, his expression as good-natured as always. "Talking about Zoe, have you told her you're leaving?"

"Not yet."

Mason rose to his feet. "C'mon, I'll go with you. She'll be less likely to collapse into an inconsolable mess if there's a crowd."

Keira choked out a laugh and stood. "Thanks, Mason. For everything."

"Pfft." He was trying to appear nonchalant, but she was relieved to see some of the joy had returned to his eyes.

The general store was on the corner closest to them. Keira was only partway across the road when her subconscious registered that something was wrong. The store's lights were on but it seemed deserted. No one stood at the checkout, and Zoe was nowhere to be seen.

Mason hadn't noticed. He was watching a group of children chasing each other near the fountain. She tapped his arm to bring him to a halt and nodded toward the window.

It took him a second to register what was wrong, then his expression darkened. A faint, nasally voice made its way through the plated glass, too muffled for the words to be recognizable.

"Stay here," Mason said, pushing through the door.

Something in his tone unsettled Keira. She lightened her footsteps as she followed him inside. Instinct told her to keep to the shadows, so she did, ghosting along the edges of the shelves.

The voice sounded clearer inside the store. It seemed to be coming from near the freezer section at the back, and its familiar, sneering cadence sent disgust writhing through her stomach.

"Honestly, I feel bad for her. The rest of her kids are overseas, right? The only support she has left is you, her least favorite. It would almost be less stressful to go through treatment alone."

Keira slipped past Mason and looked around the shelf. Partway down the aisle, leaning against the chiller unit and casually examining a carton of orange juice, stood the well-dressed man who'd bumped into Keira the previous day. His glossy, styled blond hair obscured his face, but she could easily picture his contemptuous expression and pale-blue eyes.

Just beyond him, Zoe's face was twisted into a mask of hatred. Her fingers were clenched into fists at her sides, and veins stood out on her neck. She kept her eyes resolutely on the floor, but they were swimming, the moisture threatening to tumble out and drag tracks of black mascara with it.

"Though I'm sure they'll come back for the funeral," the man said, flipping the carton around to read the ingredients. "So you can look forward to that pretty little family reunion within the next six months. That's how long Dad says she'll last. Oh, does this have added sugar? How trashy."

He tossed the carton aside. It exploded as it hit the floor, spraying orange juice across the tiles and the lowest shelves. Zoe flinched.

"*Gavin.*" Mason moved from behind the shelf, startling Keira. His voice, normally cheerful, had become deep and cold. He seemed to gain extra inches to tower over the other man as he moved to stand beside Zoe. "Pay for that juice and leave."

Keira slipped forward to stand at Zoe's other side. Zoe looked startled, but her expression had lost the awful, helpless anger. Keira took her hand and squeezed.

Gavin took half a step back and flicked his bangs as his eyes darted over them. He clearly hadn't expected company, but he recovered his smirk quickly and directed it toward Mason. "Oh, you're still hanging around town? I thought you'd moved on already." His eyes slid toward Keira, and his smile grew. "And our town's newest recluse. How charming. She looks like a frightened little mouse."

Mason shifted forward to block Gavin's view. "I mean it," he said. "You have until I count to five to get out of here."

"What happens if I don't?" Gavin leaned forward, his expression darkening. "You gonna fight me, Corr? See if I don't drag you through court for assault. Then you'd never get to be a doctor, not that you deserve the title anyway."

Mason's voice held a deep, dangerous rumble. "One. Two. Three—"

Gavin stepped back and raised his hands. "Whatever. You're not worth my time. I'm going. Have fun playing with your reject buddies. I hope they make you feel better about how much of a disappointment you turned out to be."

Mason snorted as he turned toward Zoe and Keira. "Better than yours. At least my father didn't need to bribe my way into college."

Gavin's retreat came to a sharp halt.

Mason, unconcerned, focused his attention on Zoe and gave her shoulder a squeeze. "You okay?"

Keira kept her eyes on Gavin. The tense, anxious sensation she'd felt when she first met him prickled at her skin, and her instincts screamed for her to be wary—he was no longer a null threat. Gavin glared at Mason's back. A muscle jumped in his throat, and blotches of color stained his cheeks. Something moved behind his eyes: a decision being formed. One hand twitched. A small, shiny-silver object appeared in it.

Knife. Keira's pulse kicked up. Mason had his back to Gavin. He wouldn't be able to move in time. Gavin was already stepping forward, hand rising to slice the blade across Mason's shoulders—

She responded on instinct. One hand smacked into Gavin's outstretched wrist, redirecting the knife toward the boxes of cereal on the shelf. Her other hand came up and stabbed into his neck, crushing his windpipe. Her knee connected with his stomach. He gagged and keened forward. With his balance thrown off, it was all too easy to sweep her leg behind his and send him crashing to the ground.

He landed in the spilled orange juice with a wet, smacking sound. The knife bounced off the cereal and clattered to the floor. Boxes of cornflakes tumbled from the shelf to scatter around him.

Keira took a reflexive step back to keep herself out of his reach, but her opponent was helpless. He curled into a fetal position, one hand clasped around his throat and the other to his stomach as he pulled in whimpering breaths.

The shop was perfectly silent. Mason looked from Gavin to the knife to Keira. With a faint note of surprise tinging his voice, he simply said, "Oh."

Zoe, meanwhile, grabbed Keira's arm. Her owl-like eyes were still rimmed red but had widened in awe. Color flooded into her face as she grinned. "Freaking. Amazing."

CHAPTER 22

GAVIN LAY CURLED INTO a ball, his expensive shirt soaking up the orange juice he'd spilled, moaning as he writhed between boxes of cornflakes.

Keira swayed. Taking down Gavin had brought back the thick, sickening emotions from her first encounter with him. Her hands felt dirty, like they were caked in tacky oil residue. Her mind buzzed, warning bells chiming, and it was a challenge to breathe deeply enough.

Mason put a hand on Keira's shoulder to steady her and cleared his throat. "Hey, Zo? The store has a back room, right? It might be an idea to get away from here for a minute."

She blinked, then beckoned. "Yeah, of course, this way."

They slipped through a small metal door at the back of the store, and Keira only let herself breathe more deeply once it had closed behind them. The back room turned out to be a small, dim office space. The single bulb hanging from the ceiling was enough to illuminate two desks and stacks of boxes packed along the wall. Mason pulled a folding chair out from the desk and placed it next to Keira, nodding for her to sit.

He carried a package of chocolate cookies under him arm; he must have grabbed them on the trip through the store without Keira noticing. He tore open one end and shook two out, which he placed on the desk beside Keira.

"For the shock," he explained.

"I'm okay." Her hands were shaking. She forcefully tucked them into her pockets so they wouldn't make a liar of her.

Mason held the cookie package to Zoe, but she waved them away. She was pacing, bouncing on the soles of her feet every time she had to turn in the narrow space, and her broad grin bordered on manic. "Ho-lee flipping heck. You *destroyed* him."

"Sorry," Keira managed.

"Are you kidding?" Zoe batted away the cookies a second time. "Highlight of my year. You're paying for those by the way." That last comment was directed at Mason, who resolutely shook the sweet treats at her.

He reluctantly gave up on Zoe and instead nudged the cookies closer to Keira. She caved, removing a hand from her pocket to accept the offering. "What happened back there... I didn't know I could do that."

The nearest desk was covered with scattered papers, so Mason swiped some aside to make room and perched on its edge. "It was...surprising."

"It was *fantastic*," Zoe corrected. She continued to pace,

burning up her apparently endless energy. "People will try to tell you violence is never the answer, but those people are *wrong*."

Mason pulled a face but didn't argue. Instead, he asked, "Zo, what was Gavin doing? I didn't think he shopped here."

"Ooh, no, of course he doesn't. Our humble store contains too many peasants for His Royal Assness to deign to visit. Prince Gavin, Lord of Acne, gets his groceries delivered." Zoe rolled her eyes then added for Keira's benefit, "Gavin is Dr. Kelsey's son. Because his dad's oh so important, Gavin has the impression that he's equally precious by virtue of association." She glanced aside and shrugged. "And he still hates me for that time I called him a pimply faced toad in school."

"That brings me back to my question." Mason ran his hands through his hair. "What was he saying?"

Zoe's smile fractured. She rubbed the heel of her hand over her cheeks, smudging the mascara, and exhaled a humorless laugh. "Oh. That. Mum went to see Dr. Kelsey last week and…well, Gavin's a jerk. I guess secrets don't survive long in this town."

Keira turned Gavin's comments over in her mind. There had been something about treatment and a funeral in less than six months… Her insides went cold.

The light bulb painted deep shadows around Mason's eyes as he shifted forward. "Patient confidentially is a huge deal. Dr. Kelsey should never have discussed personal matters with his son. He could lose his license for it. That aside, if your mother would like to see a different GP, I have some contacts—"

"Nah, it's fine." Zoe kept rubbing at her eyes, smearing the black everywhere until she looked like a panda. "She…just needed a test. Gonna get results next week—*no, don't you dare.*"

Mason had stepped toward her, arms extended for a hug, but Zoe stopped him with a furious glare and an outstretched finger. "No. No physical comfort. You're probably filthy with germs, you repulsive plague monger."

He chuckled and obediently returned to his seat on the edge of the desk. "All right. But if you ever want to discuss anything, or if you have questions…"

"I'll be sure to get in contact never." Zoe took a deep breath, shook herself out, and finally stopped pacing. She settled into a chair opposite Keira and gave her a weary smile. "Thanks, by the way. I was this close to decking him…but that's exactly what he wanted. To get me fired. I swear that kid's missing a few screws in his head." She grimaced, then her expression brightened. "And, Keira, what the hell? I didn't know you could fight like that."

Keira managed a weak laugh. "Neither did I."

"Honestly, it might be divine intervention that you arrived in Blighty. There are *so* many people here who are in need of a good punching. I'll write you a list."

"While I can agree that Blighty has a severe lack of rampant violence, we might want to table that idea for a while," Mason said mildly. "I think, right now, it's important that we all agree on what happened to Gavin. I saw him slip in the orange juice he spilled. He probably got a couple of nasty bruises on that shelf he fell against. You saw the same thing, right?"

"O-o-oh." Comprehension lit up her eyes. "Yeah, yeah, gotcha.

He totally slipped. But it would be such a Gavin move to try and blame dear Keira. The surveillance camera in that corner of the shop has been malfunctioning lately too. But at least you and I were witnesses to his clumsiness, and we can tell the police *all* about it."

Keira covered her face with her hands, half laughing and half groaning. "You guys shouldn't be covering up for me."

"Really? Let me consult my conscience." Mason folded his arms and pursed his lips while he pretended to think, then shrugged happily. "Nope. Both my shoulder angel and shoulder demon are in agreement: Gavin slipped, and it was one of the most magnificent examples of instant karma I've ever seen."

Zoe nodded. "I doubt he'll go to the police in any case. There's no love lost between the Kelseys and Constable Sanderson. Too many noise complaints from the doctor, and not enough action from the constable."

"That's true. If he wants revenge, Gavin is more likely to enact his own version of justice." Mason's smile dropped. "Both of you, be careful. He's not a pleasant character, and apparently, he's started carrying a knife. Compound that with the rumors…"

"Rumors?" Keira asked.

Mason grimaced. "The Kelseys went through five dogs while Gavin was growing up, one after another. They either got sick or just disappeared. I'm not accusing Gavin of anything, but… that's not normal."

You felt it when you bumped into him. You know what he is.

Keira chewed the inside of her cheek before asking, "Do you think he could have hurt another person?"

"Who even knows what he's capable of?" Zoe waved a hand. "He's carrying a knife now. Psycho."

Keira wanted to press further, to ask if there had been any missing person reports or unresolved murders in the last year, but saying it out loud would sound like paranoia. Instead, she said, "It's probably best to avoid him for a while."

Zoe rose and crossed to the desk, where a large, outdated computer was half-hidden under the paperwork. She jiggled the mouse, and the monitor lit up to show a split screen of the store's security cameras. Her lips pursed as she scanned the feeds, then she pushed away from the desk. "He's gone at least. I'll get that juice cleared up before any real customers arrive. It's getting late, so you two should scatter if you want to get home before sundown."

"I'll help clean up the juice," Keira said. "You shouldn't have to deal with that alone."

Zoe threw her head back in a cackling laugh. "Oh, you sweet, pure soul, Keira. I work retail. Not even bodily fluids can faze me anymore. Trust me, juice is nothing."

"Even so..." Words failed Keira, so she was grateful when Mason stepped forward.

"You shouldn't be alone. Is there anyone you can call?"

"Oh, absolutely. I'll call Lucas if Gavin shows his face again. Gav won't cause trouble with the mayor's son there."

Keira blinked. "Lucas is the mayor's son?"

"Yeah, and a huge brat to boot." Zoe's grin was so broad that it scrunched her nose. "I'm going to miss bossing him around when his mom finally says he's done enough penitence."

"I've still got your phone." Keira rose and followed Mason to the door. "Give me a call if you need company, or even if you just want to talk, okay?"

"I'll do that, dove."

Mason clapped Zoe on the back, then opened the door for Keira. "Drink lots of water and don't overexert yourself," he said to Zoe, who shooed them out.

"Sure, whatever. Now get outta my store. You can pay me back for those cookies later."

Once they were back on the main footpath, they slowed to a stroll. Keira tucked her hands into her pockets and turned in the church's direction. "I've got some stuff to sort out, so I'd better head back. Thanks for the coffee."

He kept pace beside her. "I'm walking you home. And don't try to argue. Gavin doesn't know where you live, but it probably wouldn't be too hard for him to find out."

"I'm not worried about him. Unless—" She peered at Mason. "Gavin doesn't have goons to do his bidding, does he?"

Mason snorted with suppressed laughter. "No, thankfully he's the son of a doctor, not a gangster. But I'd be wary of him regardless." His smile vanished as they turned into the church's lane. "Gavin's kind of a prat, but I didn't think he'd actually attack me."

She nudged Mason with her elbow. "It was that jab about his father buying his way into college. Is that true?"

"Ha! Yes, and it's even worse than that. Dr. Kelsey has tried to get him into half a dozen prestigious institutes. He eventually joined the school I was attending but was kicked out for disruptive behavior before the end of his first year. It's comforting to see that money won't open *every* door."

Keira watched her companion out of the corner of her eye. He seemed just as comfortable as normal, but then, Gavin had demonstrated an ability to needle a person's vulnerabilities with shocking precision. "Sorry if it's none of my business, but…that stuff he said about you…it's not true. I don't think anyone who knows you would think you're a disappointment."

Mason smiled. "Thank you. Don't worry. I'm impervious to Gavin's barbs." He looked away, but not before Keira caught the ghost of an emotion in his eyes, something akin to regret.

She wanted to say something else—to smooth over whatever had hurt him—but they were already at the parsonage, and she knew anything she could say would be gently rebuffed. Whatever afflicted Mason was personal and private. He wouldn't share it before he was ready.

"Should I take Daisy now, or would you prefer to keep her for the night?"

They were facing the stone fence surrounding the cottage, and Keira found herself confronted by the prospect of goodbyes before she was ready. Daisy lay on the stone step in front of the door, apparently having fallen asleep there while the sun was still high enough to warm her. Keira wanted to ask to keep the cat for one more night, but that was a selfish wish. It would be best for Daisy to move to her new home before she became attached to the cottage. "I don't have a cat carrier."

"She seems calm enough that I could probably just carry her."

Keira nodded and approached the cat. Daisy roused and blinked up at her expectantly. Keira felt numb as she lifted the cat. "C'mon, Daisy. You're getting a permanent home."

She turned to give the little black creature to Mason, but she couldn't bring herself to let go. Instead, she buried her face into Daisy's fur. Purrs rumbled through her, intensely loud, and the cat licked at Keira's ear. She finally forced herself to relax her hold. "Take good care of her."

"I will. I promise." Mason cradled the cat to his chest as concern clouded his face. "Keira—"

"I'm fine." That was an atrocious lie. She felt as though her heart were being ripped out. "But you'd better take her now before I change my mind and try to smuggle her into my luggage."

Mason's smile was one of the saddest she'd ever seen. He seemed to want to say something. Instead he shook his head and gave her shoulder a gentle squeeze. "I'll be there to see you off tomorrow."

"Thanks."

She entered the cottage and shut the door but couldn't stop herself from crossing to the window. Mason had his head bent as he walked toward the cemetery's entrance. The small black cat peeked over his shoulder. Her ears pricked forward and her eyes stared, unblinking, until Keira had to slide below the window's frame to escape the cat's gaze.

Her brain knew she'd made the right choice, but nothing had ever felt so wrong.

CHAPTER 23

KEIRA GAVE HERSELF A solid hour to indulge in abject misery as she sat under the window, staring at the ceiling and blinking at threatening tears. Eventually, though, she was forced to admit she could afford only so much moping before becoming thoroughly sick of herself.

There wasn't much left to clean in the cottage, but she made herself get up and go over the details regardless. She had to be at the train station early the following morning, and the last thing she wanted was to leave a dirty house as her parting gift to Adage. She scrubbed everything that was scrubbable, washed and restacked the dishes, folded the clothes she hadn't worn, and packed the ones she would be taking into plastic bags. Then she collected her possessions to make sure none of them would be forgotten. Her assets didn't amount to much: a handful of change left over from her shopping and the mysterious photograph showing the three unfamiliar figures.

At last, there was nothing more to do. She would make the bed the following morning, but the rest of the cottage was as clean as she could get it without investing in bleach and a vacuum.

It feels so empty without Daisy.

Keira slapped her cheeks to shake herself out of the threatening moroseness. *C'mon, Keira. We already tried being miserable. It wasn't very fun, was it? How about we do something productive instead?*

That was easier said than done. She peered at the clock on the mantel. Ten thirty. Zoe had said she stayed up most nights, but there was always the risk she would go to bed early after what had happened at the general store. On the other hand, Keira needed to speak to her, and it needed to be at a time when the conversation wouldn't be easily overheard by anyone else in her house.

Torn by indecision, Keira picked up the mobile Zoe had given her and paced the length of the cottage. She couldn't afford to risk Zoe not answering. The town's resident conspiracy theorist was vital to her plan. She crossed her fingers and hunted through the preset numbers. There were three: Mason's, Constable Sanderson's, and Zoe's.

The phone had barely finished its second ring before it was answered by a breathlessly eager voice. "Keira! What happened? Did the men show up again? Government operatives? Aliens?"

"You wish." Keira found herself laughing. Zoe's fervor was a welcome relief from the despondency. "I was calling to ask a favor, actually."

"After what you did to Gavin, I'd follow you to the ends of the earth."

"Oh, okay. Well, this hopefully won't be quite as inconvenient. Are you free tonight?"

"Always and forever, my sweet honey muffin."

"Ew. Please don't ever call me that again."

Zoe's cackling laugh blared over the phone. "Okay then, my bitter bran muffin, what can I do for you?"

Keira took a deep breath. "I need your help to do something crazy."

"Oh! Good! I was worried this might be a boring request."

"No, I mean it's really, really, stupidly crazy. And somewhat illegal."

"Where will I meet you?"

She paused and squeezed her eyes closed. "I'm not joking, Zoe. We could go to jail for this."

"It's okay. I already said yes. You can stop selling me on the idea. Should I pick you up?"

"No. I'll meet you at the fountain at midnight. Wear dark clothes and bring a flashlight."

"Oooh, are we gonna rob someone? Can I suggest a target? Or, wait, maybe you're actually a pyromaniac—"

Keira hung up so Zoe wouldn't hear her muffled laughter. She'd always known Zoe would agree to help, but her friend's overwhelming enthusiasm was like food for her soul.

She tucked Adage's flashlight and the kitchen knife into her pocket, then paced the length of the cottage while she watched the minute hand inch around the clock. The unconventional sleep schedule was dragging on her, so she brewed a strong cup of tea for the caffeine. Sitting down would allow exhaustion to creep over her and lull her into its embrace. Instead, she kept on her feet, stretching her arms, and gulped the drink down while it was still hot enough to scorch her throat.

When the clock hit eleven thirty, she rinsed the mug, set it neatly in the cupboard where it would likely sit for the next few years, until Adage found another guest to place in the groundskeeper's cottage, and wrapped a scarf around her neck. She'd chosen to wear the jeans, jacket, and boots she'd arrived at the parsonage with—partly because they were already dark and sturdy, but mostly because she knew Adage wouldn't approve of what she had planned for that night, and she hated the idea of wearing his generosity while doing something that would disappoint him.

She opened the door and called over her shoulder, "Bye, Daisy," then flinched. It was hard to know whether she wanted to laugh or cry more. Instead, she pressed the door closed and turned toward the cemetery.

Mist hung thick around the stones. It shifted lazily in the wind, and she was certain the graveyard would be full if she used her second sight. She touched the muscle and felt it ache. It was still sore from the previous night, so she didn't pull on it—especially as it would be vital for her plan to work.

This is our last chance, Emma. Wish me luck.

She turned away from the graves and strode past the parsonage. Mason's prediction of rain seemed to be accurate; heavy clouds were growing across the sky, blotting out the moon and stars. Keira had to strain to see through the dark, but she didn't dare turn on her flashlight. She'd been cautious when visiting the abandoned mill, but this night's stakes would be far higher if they were caught—not just for herself, but for her friend. She couldn't take any chances.

As she reached the base of the driveway, something large and metallic on the side of the road caught her notice. The car had parked under thick trees so not even moonlight reached it, making it virtually invisible. Keira slunk back toward the bushes, lowering her body and blending into the shadows, as she stared at it. There were no houses nearby, and she hadn't seen a car parked there before. Mason's earlier worry that Gavin would want revenge came back to her. Curiosity to see if anyone was inside the vehicle burned, but the windows were tinted, and she didn't dare get any closer.

The car had been parked in such a way that no one could go along the driveway without passing it. Keira circumvented that by slinking through the shrubs and brush. She kept her feet light and her movements fluid, knowing she would be virtually invisible in the low light but still unwilling to make noise in case the car was occupied.

The shrubs thinned as she neared the florist, so she took a chance and dashed around the building's corner. With the shop between her and the car, she pressed her back to the stones and listened, waiting for the telltale sound of a clicking car door or humming engine. Nothing. If someone was in the car, that person had either fallen asleep or failed to notice her.

She turned and crept toward the fountain. Zoe already sat on the stone edge, ankles crossed and arms folded over her thick parka to protect against the cold. She was looking in the wrong direction and didn't notice Keira until she stepped onto the stone. Zoe squeaked and pressed her hands over her mouth. "Jeez, don't sneak up on me like that!"

Keira tried to shush her friend's laughter. "Quiet. We can't be seen tonight."

"Pfft. Ha-ha, don't worry about that. This town is full of old people. They're all in bed by ten at the latest."

"Keep it down!" Keira begged. She glanced back toward the florist. Beyond the shop was a mess of shadows. She could imagine a figure standing in the darkness, easily hidden, watching them. "Please! I was serious when I said we could go to jail for this."

"Oh, that wasn't a joke?" Zoe, still speaking too loudly for Keira's comfort, hopped to her feet. "This sounds amazing. Where're we going?"

Keira exhaled and took Zoe's shoulders. She knew her request was going to sound crazy. She could only be grateful that Zoe was possibly the only human on earth who would listen to—and agree to—the plan without asking a million questions. "I want to get into the Crispin property. I want you to show me where Emma died. I can't tell you why, but it's important."

"Oh *heck* yes." As Keira had hoped, Zoe seemed not only accepting of the proposal, but enthusiastic about it. "I've never seen it myself, but I've researched enough to guess where the murderizing went down. Ah, this is so cool! I'll get to see if he really planted a memorial tree."

"Please, for all that's holy, *shh*!"

As was her mode, Zoe set a blistering pace. Her footsteps were loud and echoed off the main street's buildings, creating the disturbing impression that a dozen people were jogging alongside them. Keira stayed a few steps behind, constantly scanning their surroundings for signs of motion, and her nerves were frayed by the time they reached the town's outskirts.

Even in the dim light, she could see Zoe's cheeks were flushed and her eyes were bright with excitement. She twirled midpace, flashing Keira a grin. "Y'know, for a while, I was worried you'd turn out to be a huge stick in the mud. But you're actually really cool."

"No, sorry, your first assessment is probably pretty accurate." Even though they were leaving suburbia and the empty farmland was outpopulating the houses, Keira still kept her head low and her eyes moving. "I promise you this is very out of character. Let's just pretend I've gone mad for the next couple of hours."

Zoe snickered. "No, with superhero fighting moves like what you employed against Gavin earlier, I bet you used to be something cool like an assassin or a professional boxer or part of a government division that's so secret that not even its own members know about it."

Keira didn't respond. She doubted any of Zoe's guesses were accurate, but she couldn't claim normalcy either. She'd reacted to Gavin's attack too quickly and efficiently for her skills to have come from any sort of casual self-defense class. She looked at her fingers again. They seemed unnaturally pale in the moonlight. She squeezed them into fists, felt their power, then relaxed them again. *These hands might have committed crimes. Might have hurt people. Possibly even killed.*

The idea was too uncomfortable to contemplate. She raised her head to see they were nearing the copse of pine trees that surrounded the Crispin property.

Zoe nodded toward the woods. "There's no wall at the back of the house, which is where we want to get to, but it means going through the forest. You up for it?"

"Yeah. I have a flashlight, but it's probably better if we don't turn it on until we're—" The final words—*off the road*—died on her tongue. While she'd been distracted staring at her hands, a figure had appeared on the path behind them.

It was after midnight; there was zero chance the stranger's presence was a coincidence. Keira froze, her mind spinning through possibilities: Drag Zoe into the forest and hide? Try to bluff her way out of the encounter? Run for a farmhouse? Prepare to fight?

Then recognition hit her. The figure was still too far away to see distinctly in the wan light, but the gait was familiar. Keira's heart skipped a beat. "Oh…crap."

"What?" Zoe, who had been digging her own flashlight out of her jacket pocket, looked up, and saw the figure. "Did you invite someone else?"

"No. But he came anyway."

Mason's long cloak swirled around his legs as he neared them. His expression seemed strangely impassive in the dark, but his sharp green eyes glittered despite the shadows cast by his brows.

Zoe clicked on her light as he neared them. Mason stopped

at Keira's side, put his hands in his pockets, and glanced between the pair. "Bit late to be touring the countryside, isn't it?"

Damn it. Keira clutched for some explanation that might make sense to him, but she came up empty. Unlike Zoe, the simple excuse of "I wanted to see where Emma died" wouldn't fly with Mason, and he would think she'd gone insane if she started talking about ghosts. The best she could hope for was a diversion. "I could say the same to you. What're you doing out here?"

"Following you," he said simply.

She frowned. "Wait—were you in the car?"

"Yep. I was having trouble sleeping, so I thought I'd stand guard in case Gavin showed up. Imagine my surprise when I saw you coming down the driveway." He tilted his head and raised one eyebrow. "Then imagine my escalating surprise when you seemed to vanish into thin air. I eventually walked into the town in search of you…and followed Chatterbox's voice."

"Oops." Zoe gave an apologetic shrug.

Mason's gaze didn't leave Keira's face. He seemed to be trying to read her, but his expression was still too restrained for her to know if he was disappointed by what he found.

She licked her lips. "I really appreciate you keeping an eye out for me, but you can go home. I have something I need to do with Zoe."

"It's going to be dangerous, isn't it?" His tone was gentle, but she still felt knots squirming in her stomach.

"Not unless you consider Dane a threat, which I personally don't," Zoe unhelpfully supplied.

Both of Mason's eyebrows rose. "Ah. You're going to Crispin House, then. Am I allowed to know why?"

Keira grimaced. There was no way to play their outing off as a casual stroll any longer. "I want to see where Emma died." *There. Now he'll try to talk us out of it or threaten to call the police or go through a spiel about how disappointed he is or…*

But Mason didn't speak for several long beats. His eyes roved over Keira's face, their intensity sending prickles up her spine. Then, at last, the unreadable expression broke into a lopsided smile. "Can I come?"

"Huh?" She blinked at him. "Sorry, I mean…huh?"

He shrugged. "You don't have to give me your reasons if you really don't want to. But I suspect you have a good cause. And maybe I need a bit of an adventure after these last few months of doing nothing of significance. So yeah, to heck with it. I'm along for the ride."

She glanced toward the trees surrounding Crispin House. "I won't sugarcoat it: this is both risky and stupid. Are you sure you want to come?"

"If you'll have me. Like I said, I couldn't sleep. And"—he shot her a sheepish grin—"I'd be lying if I said I wasn't a tiny bit curious about the house."

Keira could finally breathe again. She glanced at Zoe. Her companion shrugged, indicating the choice was hers, so Keira smiled. "Yeah. Definitely. Let's go."

CHAPTER 24

KEIRA PULLED OUT HER flashlight but didn't turn it on. They slipped into the forest, with Zoe leading the way, her light bobbing across the dead, spiky branches blocking their path. Keira followed closely, and Mason was just behind her. Zoe continued to stomp through the leaves with very little concern for how much noise she was making, but at least Mason seemed to know how to be subtle. He was larger and heavier but made far less noise than Zoe.

A dozen paces into the forest, it became impossible to see, and Keira was forced to use her flashlight. The woods were untamed and had no man-made paths.

The group slowed their pace as the flat ground became consumed by indents, protruding roots, and fallen trunks. The instability forced them to test almost every step before trusting their weight to it, and the stress was starting to fray Keira's already-tired nerves.

Zoe led them straight for several minutes, then she took a sharp right. The disorienting, twisting path around the trees had thrown off Keira's sense of direction, but she thought they were moving parallel to Crispin House.

At last Zoe turned right again, leading them back toward the house. The forest began to thin, and Keira clicked off her flashlight. Zoe kept hers on.

"I'll point it at the ground; stop worrying," she whispered when Keira nudged her shoulder. "It must be one in the morning by now. There's no way Dane's still awake."

Keira grudgingly let it be.

As they neared the edge of the forest, something cold and wet hit Keira's face. She wiped it off, but it was quickly followed by another drop. The rain had started. *We'll be wet before we get home. Hopefully, this won't take long.*

She stepped through a final row of trees and found herself in the fabled Crispin garden. With the moon blocked by heavy, roiling clouds, Zoe's LED flashlight provided the only light. Its refracted beam brought a grisly maze of overgrown plants, collapsed stone seats, and upturned monuments into stark relief.

Zoe whistled, and Keira clamped a hand over her friend's mouth. "Please. Be. Quiet."

"But it's so cool!" Zoe spoke through Keira's fingers, breathing moist air onto her palm, and Keira pulled it away with a grimace.

Mason appeared at her side and bent low so she could hear his whisper. "I don't know how true they are, but I've heard rumors that Dane suffers from insomnia and takes long walks during the night. You might want to make this quick."

She nodded and turned back to Zoe. "Where was Emma killed?"

"Hmm." Zoe raised her flashlight to scan the property, and Keira had to stop herself from forcing the beam back down to the ground. Too much light or motion could stir the house's occupant, but on the other hand, Zoe couldn't lead her to the cold crime scene if she was blind.

Keira tried to regulate her breathing and tell herself the chances of being caught were relatively low, but she could already feel her limbs preparing her to flee. She flexed her hands to stop the nervous energy from overflowing into irrational actions.

"I saw the photos put in as evidence," Zoe whispered. "And I thought I could guess the scene of death based on them, but wow, a lot's changed in forty years. Can you believe this used to be a luxury property? They had a dedicated gardener to trim the hedges and stuff. Now it's like some postapocalyptic-scape, just with plants instead of collapsed buildings."

The metaphor was awkward, but Keira couldn't argue with it. As the flashlight skimmed over the yard, she saw sprawling shrubs as big as a car, flowers that had spread outside their garden beds, a stone statue of a Grecian woman with both arms lying crumbled at her feet, and a dry water fountain with decades' worth of leaves in its basin.

"It was near the house..." Zoe chewed on her thumbnail as she muttered to herself. "There was some sort of stone structure near it. Like a wall or something. And a garden bed just beside her body."

More drops hit Keira's exposed skin. She squinted against the thin rain as she looked up at Crispin House. Bleak, decaying, and sad, the mansion towered above them. Lightning crackled in the distance, silhouetting the building for a fraction of a second, and Keira shivered as the thunder shook the air. "Do we need to get closer to the house?"

"Yeah." Zoe's smile was brave, but a hint of uncertainty glinted in her eyes. "The left side, I think."

They moved forward as a unit. Although the garden was severely overgrown, it seemed to be frequently visited. Dirt tracks threaded between the plants and around the trees, showing where a lifetime of pacing had worn down the grass. It was all too easy to imagine Dane, alone, possibly deranged, spending his days in the wild plot.

"I think…" Zoe stopped twenty paces away from the building. She looked from the protruding wing of the house to a line of stones showing where a garden's border had once existed, then to a young elm growing ahead of them. "I think this is it."

Keira's breath was quick and shallow. She tucked her flashlight back into her pocket and stepped forward.

In the mill, touching the chair Frank Crispin had stood on had shown her his death. She hoped the experience hadn't been an abnormality and that it wasn't tied to a physical residue such as a fingerprint that could be erased by exposure to the elements. If she was right, standing where Emma had died should show her the girl's demise—and the killer's identity.

"This must be it." Wonder was audible in Zoe's voice. She'd apparently forgotten her anxiety as she approached the tree. "They really did plant a memorial. That's so cool."

It's twisted. Keira's heart fluttered like a panicked bird as she reached toward the tree.

"Keira?" Mason's whisper was sharp as it cut through the cold air. "I think I saw something."

No, not yet. Not when I'm so close—

Her fingertips touched the bark. Something subtle hummed through the tree, like faint static, and prickled her skin. *Show me.* She closed her eyes and inhaled. *I want to see.*

When she opened her eyes, she was no longer surrounded by black shadows and a shaking flashlight beam. Instead, the day was overcast and crisp. Something yellow shifted behind Keira, and she turned to see a woman poised just a couple of paces away.

Emma looked cold in her sundress. Color filled her cheeks as she yelled. Standing opposite was a balding, heavyset man in an expensive but old-fashioned suit. *George.* His hands were stretched wide as he bellowed at her. The argument was vicious, but neither voice was audible to Keira.

She blinked. Emma slapped George. The older man stumbled backward, hit the ground hard, and grimaced. The pained squint morphed into fury as he extended his hand, and the ring-wrapped fingers fastened over one of the stones bordering the garden.

Another blink, and Emma was fighting desperately, mouth open in a scream, as the stone was brought down over her temple. She crumpled to the ground and raised a hand to the blood dripping through her flaxen hair. Her eyes widened as George threw himself toward her.

Keira didn't want to see any more. She squeezed her eyes closed, trying to block out the sights, but they flashed across the backs of her eyelids. The stone came down again and again and again, crushing the skull, sending bone fragments flying. Emma's struggles failed after the third blow, but George didn't stop. He kept beating until her head was pulp.

When George pulled back, sucking in ragged gasps, his face was wet with blood and sweat, and clumps of hair clung to the stone in his hand. He stared at it, appearing stunned at the sight, and dropped it to the ground. He turned his gaze to the body at his feet. Then, very slowly, he rotated to look at the garden. The ground had been recently turned; a shovel still protruded from the dark earth.

Keira inhaled sharply as the vision faded. She stumbled backward, and warm arms enveloped her.

"Deep breaths," Mason urged. "Tell me what's wrong."

"Just…just surprised," she managed.

"We need to leave. Quickly. Can you walk?"

Not trusting her voice, she nodded emphatically. Her legs felt like they were made of paper, but she knew their muscles would carry her.

Mason kept his arm around her as he drew her down the path leading toward the woods. "Zoe," he hissed. "Turn the flashlight off."

"I can't see without it!" she whispered back.

Something cold was running down Keira's face. *Blood,* her mind, still full of the images of Emma's death, suggested. She touched a finger to the substance and realized the clouds had begun to release their burden in earnest.

"Turn it off." Mason's voice was tight and urgent. "We're not alone."

With a click, the light disappeared. Being blind in the overgrown garden made her sick with fear, and Keira reached for her other senses. Mason's arm across her shoulders felt firm, warm, and good. She reached up to hold his hand, and he tightened his fingers around hers. It was enough to quiet some of the panic dancing through her mind, and she tried to feel out their surroundings by sound and touch alone.

The most persistent noise was the low, droning drum of rain hitting the ground, the plants, and the house. Interspersed through it was her companions' breathing. Mason's was deep but quick; Zoe gasped in short, ragged breaths. And then Keira could sense the texture beneath her feet. She could feel the ground turning from compacted dirt to spongy grass and weeds. She snagged Zoe's sleeve with her spare hand and redirected both of her friends back to the path.

The audio was her best clue, so she focused on the different cadences of the falling rain. It was harder behind them, where it pinged off the slate roof. Ahead was softer, where it hit and ran through a forest of trees.

We're not far from the woods.

Then there was another sound. It was so faint that Keira

almost didn't pick it out from among the rainfall, but it was unmistakable: crunching gravel just ahead.

She pulled her companions to a halt, released her hold on Zoe, and reached into her back pocket. Mason's fingers tightened over hers in a silent question. She couldn't answer. Instead, she raised her flashlight and turned it on.

Dane Crispin's eyes shone like an animal's in the light.

CHAPTER 25

KEIRA PARTED HER LIPS, but her mouth was too dry to speak. Dane Crispin stood in their path, twenty feet away, his thin face appearing bleached white in her flashlight beam, his eyes glittering from behind the curtain of wet hair. Then he shifted. Something long and metallic rose into the light's circle.

"Run!" Keira cried, pushing her companions toward the woods. They broke into a dash, splitting around the wild man, stumbling over and through the bushes. The rifle cracked, loud enough to ring in Keira's ears. She flinched, but Dane's aim had been wide.

"Back to town," she called, praying that both of her friends would hear and understand her. "Get inside a house. I'll find you later."

"What—" Mason started, but Keira speared off before he could stop her. She heard him call her name but didn't look back before plunging into the forest.

Keira's flashlight was the only light in the dark night. She let her feet hit the ground heavily and slapped her arms through the branches as she ran, making as much noise as she could. It worked. Dane's footfalls were loud as he hunted after her.

Another gunshot. Keira tucked her head low and lengthened her strides to put more distance between them. It would be hard for Dane to hit her while they were running, but it wasn't impossible either.

She turned right, leading Dane away from the town. The thick forest made running difficult; branches caught on her clothes and scratched at her face. The scarf became a liability—a potential noose around her neck—so she pulled it over her head and discarded it.

Lightning cracked. Its glow flashed through the forest, submerging the vegetation in the surreal light and temporarily blinding Keira. She gasped as she misjudged her footing and stumbled over a branch. The rain made the leaves slippery. She skidded down an incline. Her ankle twisted on the uneven surface. Hot pain shot through her leg. She bit back a scream and curled into a ball as she landed. The flashlight painted a halo of light on the leaves above, so she turned it off and let the inky black night surround her.

Hide, her instincts said. She huddled as small as she could and breathed through her mouth. Her quick pace had put her well ahead of Dane; if she was lucky, he would continue to barrel through the woods blindly. She could wait until he was well gone, then creep back to town.

To her horror, the pounding footsteps slowed to a careful walk. He was angry, but not enraged enough to be careless.

He saw your light go off. He knows where you are. You can't stay here.

The rain continued to pour on the forest ceiling. Its drum was just loud enough to drown out the crunch of leaves as Keira rolled onto her hands and knees. Her ankle felt as though it were on fire. She tried rotating it and was relieved when it moved. The sprain was bad, though, and trying to run again would risk fracturing it.

I can't stay here. I can't run. I guess the only option left is to creep.

She rose into a crouch and began threading her way through the trees. Each step was like a knife through her foot, but she shoved the pain as far back in her mind as she could and closed a door on it. All she focused on was moving as quietly as possible until she was out of Dane's path. The rain dripping through the boughs was heavy and cold; she doubted Dane would spend more than an hour looking for her, and as long as she remained quiet and kept her flashlight off, the only way he could find her would be to physically bump into her.

Something clicked, and suddenly, the woods filled with light. Keira flattened herself behind a tree, her heart thundering. She wasn't the only one who'd brought a flashlight.

The beam sliced through the dark as it panned across the forest. It skimmed over the tree that shielded her and continued to move.

Damn it. Hiding was no longer an option; the forest was dense, but not dense enough to conceal her when Dane had a light. Keira lowered her body and slunk between two trees. As she moved, she tried to stay aware of what shapes would block her from his sights or give her cover. It was harder than she would have thought. Most of the trees were too narrow to fully shield a human form, and the shrubs weren't thick enough to hide behind.

Dane remained eerily silent. She'd half expected him to call to her, but he hadn't said a word. Even his breathing was inaudible; the flashlight was her only way of gauging how far behind he was. And it wasn't very far at all.

The gun fired. Chips of wood flew off one of the trees to Keira's right. She could no longer afford to move carefully and broke into a run.

Her foot hurt more than she could have imagined, but it carried her weight. She tore through the trees, head down and lungs aching. Although she moved as quickly as her body would allow her, she no longer had a speed advantage over her pursuer. His footsteps were close—and gaining with every pace.

The trees cleared ahead. The open area would give him an easy shot at her, but there was no alternative. She burst out of the forest and into a field of weeds. The plants grew high around her thighs, snagging her legs and slowing her further. She compensated by leaning forward and lengthening each step. That was a risk with a sprained ankle, but her desire to keep her body bullet free won out.

A tall, dark shape appeared ahead. *A house? Will Dane follow me if I force my way inside? Wait…no. Not a house. The mill.*

The vast brick building seemed deeply threatening with rain pouring down its sides. It was her best hope, though, and Keira redirected her path toward it. Gunfire came from behind her—three shots—then fell silent.

She reached the building and ran along its brick wall, praying Dane didn't know where to find the secret entrance. Her ankle nearly collapsed again as she took the corner too quickly. The rain was getting in her eyes, making it hard to see, so she pressed against the bricks for a second to wipe her vision clear. No pounding footsteps chased her, and she thought she knew why. The field surrounding the mill offered no cover. Dane would see her if she tried to run back to the forest. Most likely, he believed he could trap her at the mill and take his time hunting her.

He's not wrong.

Her options were few—and becoming fewer with every passing breath. Keira followed the mill's side toward the stack of crates and barrels leading to the broken window. The wood groaned as she climbed it but held her weight as she wiggled her torso through the narrow opening. Inside, the mill was perfectly black. She could guess how far away the floor was, but there wasn't much she could do to prepare for the impact as she fell into the pile of rotting wool.

She lay on the floor for a moment, trying to slow her heart, breathing deeply despite the wretched smell. The mill's emotional imprint weighed on her like a second gravity, but she pressed it back before it could overwhelm her. Everything was silent. She looked toward the window. For a moment, she could barely see the frame's outline, but then a flicker of light appeared through it, quickly growing nearer.

He's coming.

Keira rolled off the wool. She reached for the muscle behind her eyes, pulled on it, and whispered, "I need somewhere to hide. Please…can you help me?"

The room remained black. Keira strained further, trying to see the spirits she knew surrounded her, but the transparent beings seemed to be just as vulnerable to the blotting effects of night as everything else in the world.

Then something cold brushed her hand. It was so light that she would have assumed it was a breeze, except the air inside the mill was still. Keira's breath hitched. She extended her arm and felt the cold again, leading away from her and to her left.

She stumbled to her feet and hopped after it, letting the chill guide her deeper into the building. From her memory of how the space had been laid out, the spirit seemed to be leading her toward the offices at the back wall.

Then the cold moved down. Keira lowered her hand to follow it and touched the dusty wood floor. She frowned, not understanding, then her fingers found a tiny half-moon hole in the boards.

"Oh," she whispered as realization hit her. She dug her finger into the hole and pulled. The hidden trapdoor was stiff from decades of disuse, but it came away from the floor with a loud crack. Keira flinched at the noise and glanced back at the window. It was impossible to know exactly how close Dane was, but the light was bright enough to tell her she only had seconds.

She raised the trapdoor and slipped her feet inside. Lowering herself blindly into a hole caused small, horrified tremors to run up her spine. Part of her squirmed against the idea that something might be lurking just beyond her toes, waiting for her to move an inch nearer before biting. Instead, her feet touched a solid, cold surface. She tested it, then stretched her foot forward to discover that it was a staircase.

A scraping noise came from outside the window. Dane was climbing the crates. He knew how to get inside the mill.

There was no time to be cautious. Keira slid into the secret passageway, creeping down six steps, then pulled the trapdoor back into place so it was flush with the floor.

A moment later, thin blades of light shot through the cracks between the wood as Dane's flashlight passed over the room. Then a heavy thud, a grunt, and the creak of footsteps straining the ancient floor told her he was inside.

She could do nothing except close her eyes and hope. Was this secret compartment public knowledge? Had Dane come here as a child, possibly to test his courage and tell scary stories? Did he know the building well enough to search through its darkest corners?

Heavy feet passed overhead. Tiny streams of dust rained over Keira. She pressed a hand to her mouth so it wouldn't tickle her throat and make her cough.

The footsteps passed on. A door slammed open. More footsteps. Another slam. Then another.

He's searching the rooms. When he doesn't find me, will he leave?

Her chest ached from where her heart fluttered. Now that she'd stopped moving, the cold was seeping through her soaked clothing and beginning to gnaw at her core. Her fingers were numb, but she couldn't risk moving to warm them.

The footsteps came to a halt at the opposite end of the building. For a silent moment, the light skimmed over the floor above her hiding place, then the steps jogged in her direction.

Sudden panic hit Keira. She'd been dripping wet when she entered the mill; she must have left a trail of water leading to the trapdoor. If he looked closely enough, he would surely find the finger hold that had let her pull the boards up.

She considered moving farther down the stairs, but the risk of making noise was too great. Except for the pounding feet and her beating heart, the mill was almost perfectly silent.

Get ready to fight. Her muscles tensed, though she already knew her odds were bad. Dane had not only a height advantage but also a gun. She had a knife, but she would need inhuman speed to avoid the bullet he had prepared for her.

The footsteps were nearly at her hiding space. She could picture the grizzled man running his eyes over the trail leading from the window, then abruptly vanishing. He would see the hole any second…

Something clattered inside one of the offices. Dane froze, and the flashlight's beam arced away. Then he was running for the room, skidding to a halt…and falling completely silent.

Keira kept her hand over her mouth to muffle her breaths. Was a third person hiding in the mill? It seemed almost too perfect that something would fall to the ground at the exact moment she needed a distraction. But there were no gunshots, no words, and no sound of a struggle. *It couldn't have been a ghost, could it? The only spirits I've seen are inaudible and intangible...*

She heard nothing for close to ten minutes. Every few seconds, the flashlight passed over the secret trapdoor, sending the thin lines of light over the stone step in front of her face, then continued to scan the rest of the room. The cold was eating her, and she ached from holding the awkward pose, but she didn't dare move.

At last, Dane spoke. It was a single swear word, frustrated and angry, spat between clenched teeth. The feet stomped past her. She listened to his grunts as he lifted himself back through the window and returned to the outside world.

Don't be too eager, logic cautioned. *He could be trying to trick you into coming out.* She allowed herself the relief of shifting into a slightly more comfortable position, then settled in for a long wait.

Without a clock, she didn't know how much time passed. It felt like hours, though realistically, she guessed it probably wasn't more than twenty minutes. Her teeth were chattering, and chills raked through her by the time she decided that, Dane or no Dane, she couldn't sit there any longer. She pulled the flashlight out of her pocket and turned it on.

The stairs led down into a small brick room. It seemed to have been designed as an emergency hiding space—old Mortimer Crispin had probably commissioned it as a safe haven should he need it. Shelves lined two of the walls. The stairs took up a third, and a badly decayed bed was propped against the fourth. In the middle of the room was a table with a basket on it.

Keira knew she needed to return to town and seek out her friends, but something about the basket drew her curiosity. It was old, but not as old as the rest of the furniture, which seemed to have been installed at the room's creation.

As she scanned the shelves, she saw an assortment of items that looked no more than a few decades old. A record player with a track waiting to be put on. Empty wine bottles. A packet of cigarettes. A stack of letters.

She was freezing, tired, and not looking forward to a long hike back to civilization, but Keira knew this would be her only opportunity to visit the secret room. She lowered herself off the steps and groaned as blood flowed back into her cramped leg.

She hopped to the papers and unfolded a few. As she did, a photo fell from between two sheets and fluttered to the floor. She bent, picked it up, and shone her light on it.

It revealed two familiar faces: Emma and Frank, embracing in a photo booth. They were laughing. Keira gently put it to one side and opened the letters. A quick scan showed they were love notes, all signed by Frank.

She skimmed them, hoping for a clue that would help her understand Emma, but there wasn't much except for expressions of adoration, plans to meet late at night, and a throwaway suggestion for elopement. She put them back on the shelf and turned toward the basket.

The large wicker carrier held a dirty cloth. Keira picked up a corner to see if there was anything inside. A jumble of small white bones clattered together, and Keira drew in a sharp breath as she recoiled. Her heart lurched unpleasantly. She closed her eyes, inhaled deeply, and waited for the unsteadiness to fade.

I understand now. Oh, Emma, you poor creature—no wonder you can't move on.

There was no reason to linger in the young lovers' secret meeting room. Keira took the basket, climbed the stairs, pushed open the trapdoor, and returned to the mill's main room. She placed the wicker carrier onto one of the tables, then opened her second sight.

The spirits seemed to glow faintly in her flashlight. The man with the unbuttoned shirt stood closest and gave her a nod in greeting. Two of the female workers lingered near one of the offices, and Keira remembered how an object had clattered to the floor to draw Dane's attention away from the trapdoor.

Poltergeists, Keira's subconscious whispered.

"Thank you," she said, and she bowed to the spirits. "I don't know how I can ever repay you."

The man's smile widened a little. He extended his hand, palm outward, in gentle reassurance.

Keira dropped her second sight. She wished she could stay with the mill's spirits longer, but the cold was starting to become a serious problem. She reached into her pocket. Zoe's phone was wet from the rain, but miraculously, it powered on. The battery was near dead, so Keira went straight to the preprogrammed numbers and selected Constable Sanderson's.

Mason had said the policeman would answer his mobile at any hour, even during the middle of the night, and Keira sighed with relief when that proved true. The voice sounded sleepy, disoriented, and more than a little irritated. "Wha? Wha tha hell is it?"

She doubted the constable would be able to recognize her voice if he ever met her again, but she lowered it an octave just in case. "I have important information. Please listen carefully."

"Who the hell is this?" She could hear sheets rustling. He sounded a little more alert, at least.

Keira turned to look at the basket and spoke slowly and clearly. "You need to come to the old Crispin mill. I've found an infant's remains."

CHAPTER 26

WITHOUT WAITING FOR CONSTABLE Sanderson's arrival, Keira crawled out of the window and shuddered as the deluge of rain poured over her still-wet clothes. As she walked toward town, the awful scenario played through her mind, so clear and so obvious now that she'd seen the missing puzzle piece.

The secret room under the mill had been a meeting place for Emma and Frank. They must have spent dozens of evenings there, safe from the prying eyes of the town and George's disdain. Emma and Frank's child would have been conceived there.

Frank probably hadn't known he was going to be a father. Perhaps Emma herself hadn't even known on the fateful night when their secret wedding was foiled.

After Emma's parents accepted the bribe to remove their daughter from town, Emma had given birth hidden somewhere in the country, far away from society. She hoped that Frank would come to find her. But Frank, swayed by his father's iron will and unaware that he had a child, stayed in Blighty. After the better part of a year spent away from her fiancé, Emma came to the conclusion that fate expected her to take her future into her own hands. She bundled her child into a basket and followed the back roads to Blighty.

Bringing a baby onto the Crispin property while George still reigned was too risky. Instead, Emma had stopped by Polly's house. She must have intended to leave her child with her best friend while she visited Frank. But Polly didn't answer the door, and Emma didn't trust Myrtle enough to reveal her secret.

The mill's hidden room offered an alternative. To Emma, it must have seemed like the best solution. Somewhere safe to hide her baby until she could reach Frank and bring him to meet his child.

But she never found Frank. She met his father instead, and the result had been far more horrific than anything she could have prepared for. Keira had no idea what words had been exchanged prior to the murder, but she suspected that Emma had revealed the truth. She might have thought George's iron heart could be softened if he knew he had a grandchild. She'd been wrong.

To George's mind, Emma had sullied his family's lineage. He murdered her in retaliation. And his pride had been so strong that he'd accepted a life in prison without breathing a single word about the secret baby.

Keira closed her eyes in grief at the idea of the child perishing alone in the basement. She hoped it had been quick; Blighty's temperature dropped alarmingly at night, and it was probable Emma's baby had not survived until morning.

Emma's family could have told the police about the child, but they had never been found. Depending on how remote their new home was, they might not have even known their daughter was dead.

Even when Frank hung himself in the mill—directly over the room where he'd shared so much time with Emma—the secret trapdoor had not been found. And Emma was still chained to Blighty cemetery, knowing that her child's remains went unrecovered.

Keira shook herself out of the unpleasant thoughts as she reached the main road. Drawing attention to herself would be unwise. Even if Dane wasn't still hunting for her, she didn't want to bump into the constable if he responded to her call that night. She switched the flashlight off and waited for her eyes to adjust to the night. Indistinct shapes rose from the gloom as she moved alongside the road, keeping near to the woods so she could vanish into them if she heard or saw anyone coming. The only way she could be caught was through ambush.

She prayed Mason and Zoe had made it back to town okay. Her phone's battery had died as she'd finished her call to Sanderson. She only hoped that they weren't still on Dane's property.

They'd better not be; I kept Dane away for nearly an hour. She rubbed strands of wet hair out of her face and picked up her pace despite the aching ankle. *They might be waiting at the fountain, or even at my cottage.*

She didn't know what the time was, but her gnawing exhaustion suggested somewhere around three in the morning. Eventually, the empty fields were swapped out for houses. Then the houses became shops, and she was back on Blighty's main road. She still kept to the shadows, even though the streets were empty.

Keira tried not to dwell on her friends' conspicuous absence. She'd told them to get indoors; they were probably in a house, waiting for dawn. She passed the florist and followed the lane leading to her cottage. Mason's car had disappeared from the base of her driveway. She let herself relax a little. He, at least, had made it back.

If they're not waiting at the cottage, I'll recharge the phone and call them. Then I'll have the hottest shower of my life and sleep for an eternity. She blew out a breath, and the wind snatched away the cloud of mist. *It was the wrong choice to let Mason take Daisy. I'd give almost anything to have some company tonight.*

She'd reached the part of the lane that passed near the creek, and Keira watched it tumble behind its bordering vegetation. The starlight-tinted water was almost hypnotic. Something small tugged at the back of her awareness, and Keira slowed to a halt. Exhaustion had made her lower her guard as she neared home, and it took her a moment to realize what had unnerved her.

I'm not alone.

She turned and dropped in the same motion. A fist arced toward her. It carried a wickedly sharp blade. She dodged, and instead of plunging into her, the knife scraped her shoulder.

Keira retaliated with a jab into her assailant's torso. Her fist hit him squarely in his chest, forcing him back, but robbed her of her balance. Her ankle, already weakened, turned, and she collapsed into the dirt.

But she knew who her attacker was. In the instant her fist had connected with him, the familiar sense of dread flowed through her, leaving her feeling both tainted and repulsed.

Gavin Kelsey straightened, one hand massaging where he'd been hit, his drenched blond hair falling nearly to his curling lips. Their scuffle in the general store had left bruises on his neck, she was pleased to see.

Pain sparked from the cut on her arm. She raised a hand to the mark. It was bleeding freely. *Apply pressure*, her subconscious said. *Stop the flow.*

"I knew it." His words were almost manic in their triumph. There was something wild about him. It was as though he was buzzing from anticipation. "I knew it would be you."

She needed to find a way to disarm him. She couldn't hurt him enough that he would go to the police, but she needed to make sure he left her alone for good.

Keira tried to lift her injured arm. It still moved, but it hurt like hell. Her twisted ankle would slow any retreat. And Gavin undoubtedly knew where she lived if he'd been waiting in her driveway.

Her options were abruptly narrowed as Gavin leaped at her. The knife was directed toward her chest. Keira slammed her open hand against his forearm, breaking his hold on the switchblade, and the metal glittered as it flew out of his grip.

She couldn't stop his momentum, though. He was on her, pinning her to the ground, his rasping, wet breaths loud in her ears. His hands scrabbled toward her throat. She grabbed them to force them away and nearly screamed.

Touching other parts of him had given her a warning, but this was the first time she'd had contact with his hands. And that, she learned, was where the stain truly resided.

Her vision flashed to black, then stark white. She was in a landscape covered in snow. In the far distance, Blighty's town lights sparkled through the frost.

A river wove through the landscape, its surface crusted over with ice. A stone bridge interrupted the snow-dampened scene. It arced across the river, a gentle slope leading toward the forest on the other side.

Gavin Kelsey strode toward the bridge, his fists thrust into his jacket pockets and his shoulders hunched. He looked younger, Keira thought, but not by much. The fuzzy mustache was missing. He kicked at clumps of snow as he followed the near-buried path through the covered fields.

The bridge was already occupied. An older man leaned over the stones, staring down at the ice as he drew deeply from a cigarette. His eyelids were puffy and his nose red, and a brown paper bag at his feet contained an unidentifiable bottle.

"Hey, runt," the man grunted as Gavin stepped onto the bridge. "Does your father know you're out here?"

"None of your business," Gavin retorted. His scowl deepened, though, and his eyes fixed on the forest ahead. "None of his either."

The man chuckled and stubbed his cigarette out on the stone near his elbow. "Last I heard, you were going to be in trouble if you were caught setting any more traps."

"I'm not. He won't know." Gavin's jaw twitched. He kept walking, passing behind the man on the bridge, but the next words slowed him to a halt.

"All right, suit yourself, runt." The man's face was haggard and tired, and his bleary eyes followed indistinct shapes moving beneath the ice. He seemed to have tuned Gavin's presence out.

A strange expression flickered through Gavin's eyes. Keira could detect resentment, and hatred, and some sort of deep, consuming restlessness. He glanced toward town. It was at least twenty minutes away by foot. No other humans disturbed the smooth, white fields. And the older man leaned far over the bridge, his weight resting on the stone wall.

"No," Keira whispered, but nobody heard her.

A wild emotion had taken over Gavin's eyes. He stared at the man's back, fists flexing at his side, then, faster than Keira had expected, rushed him.

The man gasped on a cry as Gavin's hands hit the center of his back. He grabbed for the stones he'd been resting his forearms on. His reflexes were dulled, though, and the stones were slippery with ice.

Keira wanted to close her eyes to avoid seeing what happened next, but she was powerless to look away. Shock flitted over the man's weathered face as he plunged over the bridge and toward the river below. The ice, an inch thick, broke under his weight.

He disappeared under, then reemerged, thrashing in the hole he'd created. Keira shook her head, desperate to escape the vision. The man was drunk, and his coat was thick and rapidly absorbing freezing water. He clawed at the edges of the ice but couldn't find a grip.

"No," Keira said again, but there was nothing she could do. He disappeared under the ice, pulled by the current, until all she could see was the outline of something dark floating down the river.

Gavin stood at the bridge's edge, where the man had been just a moment before. His breathing was fast. A flush of color coursed over his face. And then he smiled, and a shocked kind of laughter bubbled out of him. As the streak of dark color faded into the distance, Gavin Kelsey hiked his jacket a little higher and, still smiling, turned to jog back to town.

Keira's vision blurred as spots of strange lights danced over her retinas. She came back to herself in increments. Mud stuck to her face and pain sparked through her skull as the deluge washed over her. She'd been struggling while unconscious and had managed to roll onto her stomach. Gavin loomed over her, one knee pressed into the small of her back, his hand tangled in her hair. He pulled, and she smothered a groan.

Gavin was panting, but when he spoke, he sounded ecstatic. "Not so tough now, are you?"

Keira tried to roll him off. He was heavy, and she couldn't get traction in the mud with her twisted ankle. Every time she moved, he dug his knee deeper into her back. Her arm was on fire, but she clenched her teeth and refused to let him hear her cry again. Puddles of muddy water flooded her mouth as she tried to breathe.

Gavin bent forward so he could whisper into her ear. "Dane called my dad. He said someone was on his property. I said I bet I knew who it was. And sure enough, your little house was empty."

Think, Keira. He doesn't have his knife anymore, but that doesn't stop him from being dangerous. I can't get out from under him. So what will make him voluntarily move off?

Gavin chuckled. It wasn't a pleasant sound. "You really hurt me in that hole of a convenience store. I stayed up last night with an icepack, thinking. I can't call the police, or you'd just leave town. Burning your shack down is too impersonal. But look, you had to go and make it easy for me." He applied extra weight to the back of her head. "Want to know *why* it's so easy?"

"Get your gross, greasy hands off me," she snarled.

He was so close to her ear that she could feel his breath tickle over her cheek. "Because no one cares about you. You're the wild girl who wandered in from hell knows where. If you disappear, they'll think you just up and wandered back out. No one will be worried. Most won't even notice. And your little friends can beg and complain all they like, but the police won't go looking for you. No one will ever know what happened to you."

It struck her that this must be the same train of logic he'd had on the bridge. She knew nothing about the strange man except what she'd glimpsed, but it was easy to guess that he was on the fringe of society. The perfect target for Gavin. The ideal opportunistic crime, one he had likely spent months wishing he could replicate.

Worst of all, Gavin was right—if she disappeared, very few people would notice.

His words made her realize something else, though. Gavin was stalling. He wanted to kill her, in the same way a starving coyote slinks ever closer to its prey, but when it came to the moment of action, he hesitated.

I can work with that.

She tensed up, pretending to struggle against him, and he predictably pushed her down even more firmly. She kept up the struggle for another second, then abruptly went boneless. From where he rested his weight on her back, Gavin couldn't miss the change.

"Hey, little mouse." He released her hair and slapped her face. She stayed limp. "Did you seriously faint on me?"

He hesitated for a moment, then snorted, and the weight left her back. It was all Keira could do to keep the grin off her face. Gavin hovered over her for a second, then she heard him move toward the river bank. He was going to look for his knife.

That was a bad choice.

Keira was off the ground before Gavin could even turn. She slammed into him, forcing him back, and they tumbled into the stream. Gavin's shriek choked off as his head plunged under the water.

Her cuts burned in protest, but Keira ignored them as she snatched her own knife out of her back pocket. She pushed her open palm into Gavin's throat to twist his head back and hold it still. They came to rest with Gavin lying almost completely in the water, staring up at Keira in horror. His hands were gripping the front of her jacket, half to fight her and half as an attempt to pull himself out of the stream.

Keira pressed her knife into his throat, just below her hand, and he exhaled a gurgling whimper. Because of the way she held him, he couldn't pull away from the water without cutting open his own throat, and he couldn't jerk away from the knife without submerging himself.

She gave him a second to appreciate his predicament before speaking. She kept her voice steady and enunciated slowly to be sure he understood.

"You got a couple of things right. I am wild. And I'm good at disappearing. I'm seriously tempted to use both of those traits tonight; by the time they find your remains, I'll be long out of here."

His eyes were wide circles, and his lips shook as he opened them, but the only sound he made was a strained, terrified whine.

"But you were wrong about something else. I didn't arrive in Blighty by accident. I have *work* to do here. And I know things." She leaned close enough to see his pupils contract with fear. "I know your secret. I saw what you did to the man on the bridge. Murderer."

His mouth worked, opening and closing again like an oxygen-starved fish.

"You thought no one saw and that no one would ever know. But *I* saw. I see everything."

"Please." His voice was strangled with tears. "It wasn't—I didn't—"

"Yes, you did. You were going to set traps in the forest, but you were tired of killing just animals, weren't you? So you pushed him. You left his bottle on the bridge and walked home thinking that no one would be any wiser."

He made a strange noise, something between a sob and a whine. "I'm sorry. It was dumb. I was so stupid— I never meant to— I never should have—"

Disgust coiled through Keira's stomach. She'd just accused him of taking a life, and yet all Gavin could talk about was himself. He didn't regret his actions. He only regretted being caught.

She could pay it forward. If she pushed his head just a little more, he'd be underwater. It might even be the same stream he plunged his acquaintance into—the riverbanks weren't as wide at that point, but she was fairly sure it would travel to the other side of Blighty, merging with its counterparts to form the large, steady flow that washed under the stone bridge.

Keira's hand twitched down, and the water rose over Gavin's ears. Just a little farther and his nose and mouth would be under too. A life for a life. Justice. At least a form of it.

In an instant, the anger and pain vanished. She'd told Gavin she'd been sent to Blighty with a purpose, but that had been a lie designed to intimidate. She didn't know why she was there, or who she had been before, or how many sins she herself had committed in her previous life. It wasn't her job to punish Gavin, no matter how greatly he deserved it. Knowing how quickly she had jumped to that solution left her clammy and sick.

Keira pulled his head up just enough to clear his ears, then spoke carefully to make sure he didn't miss a word.

"I'll be watching you from now on. You can't hide anything from me, and this will be your only warning. You're going to leave me alone. You won't bother Zoe or Mason again. No more traps, and no more picking fights. You're not going to cause trouble for this town."

Her hand was shaking. A bead of blood appeared at the knife's edge, and he squeezed his eyes closed.

"Because if you become a problem for me or my friends, I *will* come for you." She placed heavy emphasis on the words. "Don't you dare think I won't."

"Please," he begged again.

Keira held him there for a beat, watching the flowing stream dance around his head and pull at his hair, then she withdrew the knife and shifted away from him. His hands were still gripping her jacket, but he released her quickly and scrambled back to shore.

"Remember how much I know," she said. "Now get out of here."

He stared at her, his eyes huge and confused, his legs shaking in the mud, then he staggered to his feet and dashed into the forest.

Keira listened to him crash through the plants until his panicked, uncoordinated escape became inaudible, then she slumped against the closest tree. She tucked the knife into her pocket and pressed her hands over her face.

I wanted to kill him. Tears came, and they were very, very hard to stop. *I thought it would be a good idea to kill him.*

She dropped her hands and gazed at them. Their fingers had held the knife confidently. They'd been ready, almost expectant, of drawing the blade across Gavin's throat.

Just who am I?

CHAPTER 27

KEIRA WASN'T SURE HOW long she leaned against the tree and watched the raindrops fall from her fingertips. She was vaguely aware that time was passing. She just didn't have enough mental space to care. Eventually, the cold made its presence felt, and she looked up. Although it was still drizzling, the sun had started to rise behind heavy cloud cover. It offered enough light to see but did nothing to warm her.

Keira slipped her jacket off. Gavin's blade had sliced through both the leather and the cotton shirt underneath. The jacket could be stitched back together, but the shirt was ruined, so she tore the rest of the sleeve off and tied it around the cut. Gavin's blade had marked her just a few inches below Mason's careful dressing of her earlier injury, which struck her as remarkably convenient; it would be easy to clean and dress both at the same time. She didn't know how much blood she'd lost, but she was only moderately dizzy, so it couldn't be too bad.

The walk up the second half of the driveway felt as though it was the longest of her life. She considered stopping by Adage's parsonage as she passed, but he wouldn't be able to do much except worry, so she decided to let him sleep.

As she crossed the boundary into her graveyard, the familiar chill drew about her. The mist was thick that morning, and the space felt almost unnaturally quiet. Keira kept moving past the cottage and sought out the now-familiar row of gravestones by the forest. She stopped in front of the one that read *Emma Carthage 1955–1981*.

"Emma?" Her voice was raw and raspy. Standing took up more energy than she was comfortable with, so she let her legs buckle and dropped to her knees. Then she reached for her second sight.

An ethereal, transparent shape emerged from the mist. Emma stood behind her grave marker, her long fingers braced on the stone top, as she watched Keira. Gentle concern creased her bloody face.

"You won't believe the night I've had." Keira managed a dry chuckle. Her smile faltered. "I think I finally understand. I ended up back at the mill. I found the secret room."

Emma's eyes widened. She stepped forward, passing through her headstone, and leaned near to Keira. The sundress swirled in an invisible wind, and frost spread outward from where she touched the ground. Keira could feel the chill radiating off the ghost, and huge plumes of condensation billowed from her lips as she spoke.

"I'm so sorry. I found your baby."

Emma pressed her hands over her mouth. Liquid flooded her eyes, mixing with the blood and dripping over her mute lips.

Keira tried to smile. "I looked for her ghost. She's not there. She moved on to her next life—probably at the same moment she passed away. I called the police about her, so she can have a proper burial. But she's not on this earth anymore. I...I don't know what's in the next life, but...I suspect she'll be there, waiting for you."

Tears continued to flow, but when Emma lowered her hands from her mouth and pressed them to her heart, her lips formed a fragile smile. She spoke, and although Keira couldn't hear the words, she could read them: *Thank you, thank you, thank you, thank you.*

The spirit's form seemed fainter. Keira, thinking her second sight was waning, pulled on the muscle until it ached. But then she realized her vision wasn't at fault—Emma was fading. Her form disappeared in shreds as though she were made of a smoke that was caught up by a breeze. The spirit closed her eyes and lifted her chin. A moment later, she no longer existed.

"Oh," Keira whispered.

The clouds had started to clear, and shreds of thin sunlight struggled through. Keira, still kneeling in the mud, knew she would need to get up and return to cottage, but her limbs seemed to have mutinied and refused to respond. Her head drooped forward. Blood continued to seep through her makeshift bandage, but she didn't have the energy to care.

There's no harm in sitting for a moment, surely? I don't even feel that cold anymore. I'm sure I'd do better after a sleep...

"Keira!" The voice cut through her disorientation.

It was familiar, and Keira smiled. *Oh, good. Mason's okay.*

"Keira!" He skidded to a halt at her side. "Where have you been? I've been calling and looking for you everywhere and—oh hell, is that blood?"

"It's been a weird sort of night," she admitted.

Mason swore under his breath, then draped a warm jacket around her, followed by his arms. Keira let herself fall against him as he lifted her and cradled her like a child. "Hang on. I'm going to get you inside."

"Good, Mason," she said, and she patted his shoulder. "You do that."

Mason held her carefully, her head tucked against his shoulder, his gait quick and smooth. He inexplicably smelled like cinnamon. She closed her eyes and relaxed into him. When he tried to set her down, she grumbled.

"I know." He rubbed at her hands until sensation began to return. "I'll take care of everything. Just sleep."

That sounded like an award-winning idea, and Keira let herself slip into patchy unconsciousness. Something warm pressed against her chest. *A hot water bottle?* She wrapped her arms around it as scissors snipped at the wet clothes. Then biting pain in her shoulder made her snap back to awareness. She'd been wrapped in at least eight layers of blankets, and Mason was dabbing a smarting liquid over the cut.

"Stop it," she grumbled, trying to roll away. The blanket cocoon was too thick for her to move more than a few inches.

Mason looked pale and had dark circles under his eyes, but he still smiled. "Everything's okay. Go back to sleep."

The next time she woke, the pain had dulled to an ache and she no longer felt like a human-shaped ice block. Voices in the room spoke quietly. Keira's eyelids felt too heavy, so she let them stay closed as the words flowed past her.

Mason sounded agitated. "Even if she hadn't half frozen out there, the blood loss alone would stop her from traveling."

Adage replied, "I understand—"

"She needs rest. And I don't think she's been eating properly either. There's no way I'm letting her leave today."

"If you would just—"

"You'll have to tell that woman in Glendale to look for a different assistant."

"My dear boy, *please* listen." Adage sounded exasperated. "You're spending a terrible amount of energy arguing against a shadow. I already called Miss Wright and explained the situation. No one expects Keira to leave today."

"Oh." After a pause, Mason sighed. "Sorry."

"Now, kindly stop pacing. You're wearing holes in both the carpet and my nerves."

A chair scraped as Mason sat down. The men dropped into silence for a moment, then Mason spoke again. Unlike earlier, he seemed to be choosing his words carefully. "Let her stay here. She won't say as much, but I know she doesn't want to leave. She could live in this cottage. I'd help her find a job."

"Mason, I am awfully fond of you, but I've known Catholics

who worry less. We can discuss what's to be done once she's awake and can actually have a say in the matter."

Mason didn't reply, but Keira imagined him nodding. She was just on the edge of falling asleep again when something warm and heavy thumped against her arm. She mumbled as she turned to see the object.

Two huge amber eyes stared at her. Daisy's ears twitched, then the black cat stretched, shook herself out, and curled into a tidy ball at Keira's side.

"Hey there," Keira mumbled and extracted an arm to scratch its head. As she pulled the limb free from the blanket cocoon, she saw that a swath of bandages had been wrapped around the cut.

Mason heard her. He carried his chair from the fireplace to prop it next to her bed and nodded to the cat as he sat. "She's some kind of escape artist. When I left her at home, I was certain I'd closed every door and window in the house. I don't even know how she remembered the way back here, but she showed up barely an hour after I found you."

"Maybe she's magic," Keira murmured to herself.

The cat leaned into her hand, and when Daisy's eyes met Keira's, there seemed to be some kind of understanding inside. Then she rolled onto her back, poked one leg into the air, and began licking her butt.

Keira blew out a breath. "Ha. Maybe not."

Mason was watching her closely. "How do you feel?"

"Pretty damn fantastic compared to earlier." Everything ached, but she was warm in bed, and at least the edge of tiredness had been taken off. "Thanks for all of this by the way."

He shrugged. "It's what I do."

Adage appeared at Mason's side and wordlessly handed him a steaming bowl. The pastor gave Keira a kindly nod, then returned to the fireplace.

"Do you feel up to eating?" Mason held the bowl forward. "It's chicken soup. Adage made it."

"It's from a can, but I was responsible for heating it, so I won't refuse credit," the pastor called from his seat by the fire.

It smelled amazing. Keira took a drink straight from the bowl, then asked, "Is Zoe okay?"

"Yes and also no?" Mason laughed and ran a hand through his already-ruffled hair. "When you didn't show up in town, we both panicked a bit. Remember her theory that Dane Crispin is a vampire? She kicked through a fence so she could use the picket as a stake."

Keira pressed a hand over her mouth. "Oh no."

"Yes. She was fully prepared to storm the castle, so to speak."

"But she's okay now? She's staying away from Crispin House?"

"I called her to let her know you're okay. She said she was going to get some sleep but will come and visit later this afternoon. I suspect she wants to know what happened." His eyes darkened a fraction as his gaze slid to the bandages on her arm. "I do too."

There was no way she could truthfully explain everything that had happened. The best she could do was give him a sheepish smile. "Last night was really just a series of awful mistakes. I got away from Dane easily enough, but then I became lost in the forest, and the phone's battery ran out. I found my way back to town eventually; it just took a while."

Mason's eyebrows pulled closer together. "The cut. Did Dane do that?"

Keira hesitated. The firmness around Mason's mouth and the cold light in his eyes hinted at carefully contained anger. She couldn't tell him that it had been Gavin; that would lead to questions she couldn't answer, such as why Gavin was no longer a threat.

The man from the bridge deserved justice, but she had no evidence that Gavin was responsible—just the knowledge her second sight had given her. She didn't even know the older man's name. That thread couldn't be dropped, but she needed time to untangle it, and until then, she would have to lie. "No, this was my fault. I was carrying my knife but tripped and stabbed myself like the world's biggest klutz."

She grinned and shrugged in a *What can you do?* sort of way, but Mason's frown only deepened. He didn't believe her.

Adage appeared at the bedside and placed a hand on Mason's shoulder. "I think now would be a good time for you to go home. We can sift through the details later. But right now, Keira needs rest, and so do you."

Mason had been awake all night, Keira remembered, and he looked it. Dark shadows hung about his eyes and his expression was strained. Mason hesitated, so Keira gave his shoulder a reassuring poke. "I'm good. We'll catch up later. Go get some shut-eye, okay?"

He took a slow breath, nodded, and rose. "Call me if that cut starts bleeding again or if you feel dizzy." He retrieved his jacket, still damp from the rain, then paused at the door. "It's going to be okay. Everything is, I mean. We'll figure it out." Hesitating, he stared at the handle, then he gave Keira a weary but still warm smile. "I'll see you later."

As the door clicked closed, Adage placed a bundle of fresh clothes on the end of Keira's bed. He then returned to the little kitchen counter and filled the kettle. "Thank goodness he finally left. I'm quite fond of that boy, but he can be exhausting. Now, I would like to have a talk with you, my dear. Do you feel up to it? I'll make a cup of tea."

"Of course." Keira gave her cat a final pet, then nudged her toward the end of the bed. She quickly shimmied into the fresh clothes while Adage faced the kitchen. Mason hadn't just bandaged her arm, but bandages also covered the myriad cuts she'd earned while running through the forest, and he'd bound her twisted ankle too. A pang of fondness for him warmed her.

Adage didn't speak as he boiled the kettle and filled two cups, but when he turned back to the fire, his expression was grave. Unease coiled through Keira's chest, dampening the happy glow. *Did Mason tell him I broke into Dane's garden? Is he angry?*

Adage nodded to the fireside seats. "Come and sit where it's warm."

He sank into the plush armchair, and Keira took the place next to him. She gratefully accepted the second mug and wrapped her hands around it as she waited to hear her fate.

"I received a call from Constable Sanderson a little earlier this morning," Adage said at last. He stared at the crackling flames. Something about the pale morning light made his face seem older than it had before, as though he'd grown a webbing of new wrinkles overnight. "He wanted advice and reassurance. Apparently, he found an infant's skeletal remains in the old mill."

Keira's mind was racing, but she kept her mouth closed. Adage let the silence stretch for several agonizing minutes before he looked at her. His mouth twitched into a smile. "I don't think Mason has pieced the puzzle together yet. It's possible he never will. He's smart, but he has also grown up in a world filled with science and won't find it easy to consider options outside his established paradigms. On the other hand, my entire life is based on the idea that having faith is more important than trusting in what we can see." He sighed, took a sip of the tea, then fixed her with his sharp blue eyes. "You can talk to ghosts, can't you?"

Panic churned Keira's stomach. She didn't know where to look or what to say. *Is there any chance I could feign ignorance? Or is lying to a pastor the sort of thing that gets you sent straight to hell?*

Adage turned back to his tea. "It wasn't hard to figure out. You've been asking about Emma Carthage with far more intensity than any normal tourist would express. You were missing all night. Mason says he found you under Emma's grave. And now an anonymous woman drew the police's attention to a child's remains in the same building where Frank hung himself." The pastor's bushy eyebrows bunched up. "With bureaucracy how it is, it will take weeks, if not months, for the police to give an official finding. But it was Emma's baby, wasn't it?"

"Yes." Keira's mouth was dry. Her fingers ached from gripping the cup too tightly.

Adage sighed and sagged forward. His face contracted, and for a second, Keira was afraid he was hurt. Then he blinked, and she saw his eyes were blurred by unshed tears. "All this time," he muttered, speaking to the fire rather than her. "I'd thought she'd moved into the Lord's embrace, but all the while, she's been trapped here."

"I'm so sorry." Keira didn't know what else to say. She'd grown to associate Adage with kind smiles and a carefree personality. To see him distressed made her insides ache with guilt.

"Tell me the truth, child. Is she gone now?"

"Yes." Keira glanced toward the window. The mist had thinned, but enough of it lingered around the gravestones to cast an ethereal glow in the faint sunlight. "I think so. She didn't want to leave while she thought her baby might still be on earth. But the infant had already moved on, and now that it will have a proper burial, Emma's gone too."

Adage nodded. He lowered his cup to the floor, then leaned back in the chair. "You told me you had no memories. Was that a concealment?"

"No. It's the truth. I don't know who I am or why I can see ghosts. I just can."

Adage pursed his lips as he nodded. "Are there other spirits?"

"Yes."

"In my cemetery?"

"Yes."

"How many?"

Keira looked back at the window and pulled on the second sight. The muscle still ached, but engaging it seemed to become slightly easier each time she used it. She saw the shimmer of faint, transparent forms. "At least a dozen. Emma was the clearest. Some of the others are almost too faint to see."

"A remarkable talent," Adage said, watching his laced fingers. "I'm sure you've already considered the possibilities this ability offers. You could be a television personality. A spirit medium for hire. Even the Catholic Church might be interested in employing you; they have no small number of qualified exorcists in their ranks."

Those options had never occurred to her; she'd been too busy thinking about all the ways the gift could ruin her life. Keira tried to imagine being famous, talking to ghosts on live television or invoicing wealthy clients for séances. Even just thinking about it made her feel dirty.

Her expression must have revealed her reluctance because Adage chuckled. "Not your cup of tea, child?"

"No, thank you."

"Well, I have an offer of my own. Now, to be clear, I cannot afford even a fraction of what your talent would be worth. But I can give you this cottage to live in, dinner with me as often as you would enjoy it, and a modest weekly wage."

Keira blinked. "Sorry, do you mean—?"

"I would like you to support Blighty's spirits in moving on to the next life." Adage took off his glasses and polished them on the edge of his sweater vest. His eyes looked misty again. "I became a pastor to assist as many souls as possible, and I am proud to say I have given the task everything I have. But my ability to help people ceases the moment they die." His eyes met hers. "I can shepherd them during life, but I would like you to guide them after death."

Keira's throat was tight. Instead of trying to speak, she nodded. Her mind was too full of ideas to hold them all. Staying in Blighty. Living in the cottage that had already begun to feel like home. Keeping Daisy. Coffee with Zoe. Learning about the town with Mason.

And the ghosts. Emma's situation had been both complex and frustrating, but knowing she had gone to meet her child and her fiancé had made it worthwhile. Every ghost in the graveyard would have a reason for lingering. Some might be resolved in half a day. Others, she was afraid, might never be able to move on. But she would try. Not just for the spirits in the cemetery, but for the souls trapped in the old mill. She owed them.

"Thank you," she said at last. "I'd love to stay. Thank you so much."

"Excellent." Adage's earlier despondency faded, and one of his grandfatherly smiles returned to his face. He stood, returned his cup to the sink, and took his coat off the hook by the door. "Then I will follow the same advice I gave to Mason earlier; the details can be decided on later. For now, you need to rest, and I am overdue for my morning calls. Mildred Hobb will never let me hear the end of it."

He stopped at the door, one hand on the handle, and gave her a final, gentle smile. "I'm glad you're staying, Keira. Ghosts aside, I've grown quite fond of you."

She grinned. "Same to you."

The door closed with a solid click as the pastor left. Keira rose, put her own cup in the sink, and went to the window. Adage's pace was brisk as he returned to the parsonage. The harsh morning chill was abating, and a scattering of visitors had entered the graveyard to pay their respects to friends and family. Keira felt for the muscle, opened her second sight, and inhaled as she saw the congregation of souls. The aloof Victorian woman strode among the guests without looking at them. Two middle-aged spirits sat next to each other, not speaking but seeming to enjoy the company. A young girl darted between gravestones, playing a game of hide-and-seek that only she could participate in. More shapes, still indistinct but no less worthy of care, lingered deeper in the graveyard.

To her left, the older stones gradually merged into the forest. She would need to venture inside the woods eventually, to meet the presence that had filled her with dread on her first day in Blighty.

Then, too, were the men who had hunted her on her first night in town. She didn't know if they were still searching for her or what they wanted from her, but despite the increased risk that came with staying in Blighty, she found she didn't care. *Let them find me if they want.* She was no longer friendless, no longer vulnerable.

Daisy stretched, leaped down from the bed, and sauntered over to Keira. The little cat rubbed against her leg affectionately, then crouched and leaped onto the windowsill. Keira stroked the fur between Daisy's ears as the cat watched the graveyard with her.

Keira's heart felt so full, it ached. She owned nothing, not even her own identity, but what she did have was worth far more. She had a home. She had friends.

Most of all, she had a purpose, and she intended to give it everything she had.

ABOUT THE AUTHOR

Darcy Coates is the *USA Today* bestselling author of *Hunted*, *The Haunting of Ashburn House*, *Craven Manor*, and more than a dozen other horror and suspense titles.

She lives on the Central Coast of Australia with her family, cats, and a garden full of herbs and vegetables.

Darcy loves forests, especially old-growth forests where the trees dwarf anyone who steps between them. Wherever she lives, she tries to have a mountain range close by.

VOICES IN THE SNOW

NO ONE ESCAPES THE STILLNESS.

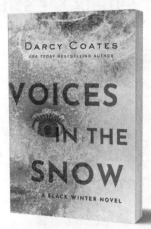

Clare remembers the cold. She remembers dark shapes in the snow and a terror she can't explain. And then…nothing. When she wakes in a stranger's home, he tells her she was in an accident. Clare wants to leave, but a vicious snowstorm has blanketed the world in white, and there's nothing she can do but wait.

They should be alone, but Clare's convinced something else is creeping about the surrounding woods, watching. Waiting. Between the claustrophobic storm and the inescapable sense of being hunted, Clare is on edge…and increasingly certain of one thing: her car crash wasn't an accident. Something is waiting for her to step outside the fragile safety of the house…something monstrous, something unfeeling. Something desperately hungry.

SECRETS
IN THE DARK

YOU CAN'T OUTRUN THE STILLNESS.

Winterbourne Hall is not safe. Even as Clare and Dorran scramble to secure the ancient building against ravenous hollow ones, they face something far worse: Clare's sister has made contact, but she's trapped, and her oxygen is running out.

Hundreds of miles separate Clare from Beth. The land between them is infested with monsters, and the roads are a maze of dead ends. Clare has to choose between making a journey she knows she might not survive, or staying safe in Winterbourne and listening as her sister slowly suffocates. At least, whatever her choice, she'll have Dorran by her side. And yet there are eyes in the dark. There are whispers in the mist. There is danger lurking in the snow, and one false step could end it all…

WHISPERS IN THE MIST

YOU WON'T SURVIVE THE STILLNESS.

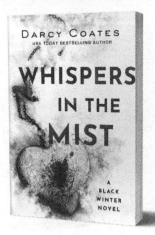

Clare and Dorran may still be alive against all odds, but relief is only temporary. Dorran is sick, and rapidly worsening. Clare fears the only way to save him lies in the mysterious Evandale Research Institute, supposedly one of the few remaining human refuges. But the research station is three days' journey away, and Clare isn't certain their small group can endure that long. Because the danger they're facing comes not only from the ravenous hollow ones...but from each other.

This terrible new world has left scars, and only some of them are physical. As Clare fights to protect the most precious people in her life, she begins to realize a horrible truth: not everyone can be saved. And sometimes the worst monsters wear a human smile.

SILENCE IN THE SHADOWS

THERE'S NO SAFETY IN THE STILLNESS.

Clare and Dorran have set their sights on returning home to Winterbourne Hall. It's a daunting journey, but vital. Humanity needs more refuges—safe areas where food can be grown without attracting the attention of the hollow ones—and the old gothic manor is their best bet.

But their home is no longer a sanctuary. It's become a trap: carefully crafted for them, lying in wait for their return. By the time they realize just how dangerous Winterbourne has become, it's already too late.

The fight for survival is far from over.